SWITCHBLADE

switch·blade (swĭch´blād´) n.
a different slice of hardboiled fiction where the dreamers and the schemers, the dispossessed and the damned, and the hobos and the rebels tango at the edge of society.

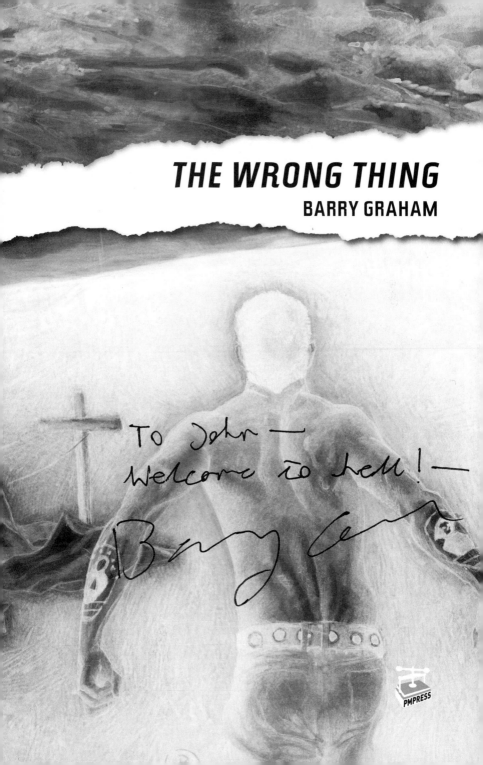

THE WRONG THING

BARRY GRAHAM

To John —
Welcome to hell! —

Barry G

PMPRESS

The Wrong Thing
By Barry Graham

Copyright © 2011 Barry Graham
This edition copyright © 2011 PM Press
All Rights Reserved

Published by:
PM Press
PO Box 23912
Oakland, CA 94623
www.pmpress.org

Cover designed by Brian Bowes
Interior design by Courtney Utt/briandesign

ISBN: 978-1-60486-451-9
Library of Congress Control Number: 2010916487
10 9 8 7 6 5 4 3 2 1

Printed in the USA on recycled paper, by the Employee Owners of Thomson-Shore
in Dexter, Michigan.
www.thomsonshore.com

for Chrissie Orr
and for the kids, all of them

"I'm a little striped skunk
Sleeping under someone's bunk
Nobody else will sleep with me
I'm as smelly as can be"
—campfire song

"If you can take being weak long enough,
it in itself will make you strong."
—Rick Bass

PROLOGUE

L isten. This is what they are saying about him:
   "The Kid? Yes, I knew him, and I know his mother and father too. The Kid sold drugs and killed people."
   "How many people did he kill? Who can say? He killed somebody when he was twelve. And he got away with it."
   "My cousin Ramon was burning a tire with his friends on Guadalupe Street. It was a cold night and they were standing around talking and trying to stay warm. And the Kid came walking up the street, Ramon said something to him, and the Kid said something to Ramon and then the Kid pulled out a knife and stuck it in Ramon's throat and ran away."
   "The Kid? I knew him. Everybody knew him. Most people were afraid of him. When a man I knew disrespected the Kid's woman, the Kid came and cut off his ears. He said that if the man testified he would come back and cut off his nuts."
   "I was living with a man, and the Kid came for him. Thank Jesus, I wasn't there—I was visiting my mother with our child . . . But my man told me what happened. He opened the door, and the Kid shot him and just walked away. My man didn't die. He's still alive. He can't move, he can't breathe, he can't piss. It all has to be done for him. He's always covered in sores from laying in the bed or sitting in the wheelchair. I didn't want to stay with him, but I did, because I didn't know how to leave him like that. The Kid took my life away."
   "Oh, yes . . . the Kid. I was never afraid of him, but other people are. Yes, they still are. They're afraid of a dead man. They think he'll still come and get them if they don't keep their mouths shut."
   This is what they are saying about him, what some people are saying about him. And it may be true. Or it may be lies. Just like the story I am about to tell you. It may be a lie, it may be the truth, or it may be both. Nobody knows. The only one who knows is him, and he

can't speak anymore. And I can't speak for him; I don't know what he would say. I can only speak of him, tell another version of the story. Not a lie, and not the truth. Just another version of the story.

Listen. This is what I am going to say about him.

ONE

The name on his birth certificate doesn't matter. You wouldn't recognize it if you heard it. When he grew up he used many different names. But all through his life he was called the Kid.

He was his parents' first-born, and they referred to him as "the Kid" right from the start. So all their relatives started calling him the same thing. As he grew up, it was how he thought of himself, whenever he did. He had a younger sister, but she was called Celeste and he was still the Kid.

Celeste never seemed to have a problem with anything. The Kid just couldn't seem to get anything right; he always had to know why things were as they were. His parents were second-generation Mexican-American, and they didn't speak Spanish, though they had the accent. They spoke the slang of the barrio they lived in. But when their son spoke the same way, they would pretend not to understand.

"What does 'ain't' mean?" his mother would ask him.

"You know what it means," the four-year-old would say.

"No, I don't," his mother would tell him.

"Yes, you do. You say it."

"It doesn't matter if I say it or not. You don't say it. The word is 'isn't.'"

The Kid would ask her why she and his father used the word if it wasn't proper. She never answered.

At age four, the Kid had a fine vocabulary of swear words. Anytime he swore, his mother would yell, "Where did you hear language like that?" He had learned by then that it was useless to answer, "From you and Daddy."

On his first day at school, the Kid was terrified. So was his mother. She was sure he would become hysterical when she left him there. Some of the other kids did. When their mothers left, they cried and screamed and said they wanted to go home. One little girl kept it up for so long that the teacher stomped her foot and yelled, "Go home, then!"

During it all, the Kid never made a sound. He didn't cry and he didn't speak. He just sat there and watched what was going on. It wasn't that he was happy—he was afraid of the teacher and the other kids, but he was too frightened to say anything. He wanted to go home, but he knew he couldn't go home and so there was no point in crying, which would just get him in trouble. He sat quietly. This is something he would do in similar situations all through his life.

His first few days at school were all the same. But things changed for him the day the teacher started teaching the class how to read. She drew the letter *a* on the board and told the class, "This is aaaahh." The Kid was fascinated. He couldn't believe it was that easy to put words onto paper, like talking to somebody. If he could read, then people he had never met could talk to him. It wasn't long before he could read easily. While the other kids were moving their lips as they read Dick and Jane, the Kid was reading novels and comic books.

He soon got tired of those. He didn't have much romance in him. He didn't want to read stories that somebody had made up, and he couldn't understand why other people did. He wanted to read about things that had happened. He loved newspapers, even though he didn't understand many of the stories. At least they had happened, and there were photos of the people they had happened to. As the Kid got older, he would scavenge in used bookstores, looking for history books. By the age of fifteen, he would own more than a hundred of them. As he started to understand the stories in the newspapers, he thought he might work for a newspaper someday, taking the photos or telling the stories.

It would never happen. The Kid wasn't a good student, not even in English. He didn't like to read the novels and plays he was supposed to read for class. They weren't true, and, even if they had been true, they had nothing to do with him. They were always about white people, and the characters usually had money. There were no books or plays about someone's mother crying because there was no money and her husband was drunk and hitting her, nothing about a brother or cousin dying of AIDS while in prison. There wasn't much of that in the newspapers either, but there was some. And so the Kid just skimmed the books or didn't read them at all. He averaged a C in English. He did better in history, scoring As and Bs. He had to learn not to argue with the teacher. He had read many history books that weren't on the syllabus, and he knew that some things the teacher said weren't true. But arguing got him nowhere, so he learned to pretend to believe the teacher, and he did quite well.

But that was as well as he did. Math bored him, and so did every other class. He never got passing grades in anything but English and history. More than anything, the Kid hated sports. He was small and frail-looking, so nobody took him seriously as an athlete, which suited him. He'd just try to keep out of the other players' way until the game was over. The Kid's best friend when he was twelve was a boy named Rodrigo. He was very fat. The two of them would hang out on the fringes of a game, talking to each other while trying to seem at least semi-involved in the competition.

One time, the class was playing basketball. One of the players was a big white boy named Gordon Ritchie. At twelve, he was as big as some of the teachers. He was popular and friendly, but for some reason he didn't like the Kid.

During the game, the Kid and Rodrigo were going through the motions, keeping a conversation going as they slacked. Gordon walked up to them. Ignoring Rodrigo, he told the Kid, "You better start playing. Or I'll get you later."

The Kid didn't say anything. He was timid about fighting, and Gordon weighed more than twice as much as he did. The Kid just nodded and moved away, but he didn't make any effort to get involved in the game.

Afterwards, the Kid was sitting on a bench in the locker room, tying his shoelaces. Gordon came in. Without saying anything, he punched the Kid in the face. "Do what I tell you in future," he said, then walked out.

The Kid lay on the bench, holding his face, bleeding from both nostrils. Some of the other guys felt sorry for him, and some of them laughed at him. Rodrigo got him some toilet paper and he pressed it to his nose. "You okay, man?" Rodrigo said.

"Yeah," said the Kid. His voice was shaking and it sounded like he was going to cry, but he didn't.

They had English class later that day. Gordon sat behind the Kid. As the class went on, the Kid sat at his desk with a pen in his hand, but he didn't write anything down. He just sat there with the pen in his hand.

Nobody saw what happened next, or else nobody admitted to it. A couple of people said they saw the Kid stand up, turn around quickly, and sit down again. But neither of those people was there at the time.

The teacher had turned her back to the class and was writing on the board. She heard something and looked around. Gordon Ritchie was coming towards her, reaching for her, whimpering. The Kid's pen was sticking out of Gordon's face. The Kid had stabbed him with it, stabbed him so hard that it pierced his cheek and impaled his tongue.

The teacher backed away from Gordon, trying to take in what she was seeing. Bubbles of blood were coming out of his mouth. Some of the children ran out of the room. Others screamed or cried. The Kid just sat at his desk, as though there had been no interruption to the class.

— * —

It would often be said that the Kid could not fight without weapons, that he was a coward when you got him unarmed and one-on-one. But few people would ever want to test that theory, because it would also be said that, having beaten him, you would have to go into hiding or else never stop looking over your shoulder. Because the Kid would be patient, and, when you least expected it, he'd pull something out of a pocket or from under a shirt, and you'd bleed.

— * —

If he was white and his family had money, the Kid would probably have been given therapy and then sent to a Montessori school. But he wasn't white, and the family was poor. So he was locked up for a while and then let out and sent to another school. And if it made any difference to him, nobody knows about it.

TWO

The Kid liked the barrio. It felt like home, even though his parents didn't give him a home, only a place to stay. He was never abused in any way that Child Protective Services could have acted on—his father rarely hit him, and his mother never did. They didn't even raise their voices to him very often.

But they didn't do anything else with him either. They never talked with him or asked him about what he was doing, his friends, or the books he was reading. All they had, they gave to his sister. The Kid had four shirts, two sweaters, one coat, and one pair of pants. Celeste had a wardrobe. The Kid's room contained a bed, a dresser, and nothing else, not even a radio. Celeste had a TV and a stereo system that their parents had bought for her on credit. There were many days when the Kid went to school without a cent in his pocket, but Celeste never had to.

The Kid didn't mind at first. When he was very young, he didn't know he was poor. He just assumed it was normal. As he got older, he began to realize that Celeste had more than he did, and that kids who didn't live in the barrio had more than his entire family. The other kids at school were afraid of him, so not many of them made fun of his poverty. One who did ended up transferring to another school out of fear that the Kid would do something to him—and, in some stories, the Kid still found him.

But the other kids didn't have to make fun of him. He felt it anyway. The worst time was when the school was showing a movie as part of a history project. The movie was free, but the teachers created the atmosphere of a movie theater, selling soda, hot dogs, nachos, and popcorn, thinking it would be more fun for the students. It was, but not for the Kid. He didn't have any money. It wasn't too bad during the movie, but afterwards, when the students were hanging out, talking with the teachers, the Kid was the only one not eating and drinking.

"Don't you have a Coke?" one of the teachers said. She was trying to be kind. The Kid could tell that she was going to offer to buy him something. But he didn't want her to know, and he didn't want the other kids to know, so he just said he didn't want anything. The teacher let it go, but she knew. The other kids had heard her, and they knew too.

The Kid was never able to ask for anything, or even take most things that were offered to him. At his first school, when he'd been friends with Rodrigo, he'd sometimes go to Rodrigo's house when the family was having dinner. He'd sit at the table with them, but he'd never eat anything. Rodrigo's mother would offer him food, and he'd always want it, but he'd always say no, that he wasn't hungry. He didn't know why he did that, but he always did.

By the age of fourteen, the Kid had more money than most of his peers. He could always find a job, though he could never keep one for long. And he was already selling drugs.

His parents never asked where his money came from, they just told him that he'd better not ever bring the cops to their door.

And the Kid was content.

He didn't mind his parents' indifference. He had never known anything else. And he was indifferent to them, and to Celeste. He didn't mind them, but he didn't particularly like them, and he certainly didn't love them. As long as he had a room in their house, they served their purpose.

He liked being in the house. He liked walking through the barrio on cold winter evenings, seeing the lights coming from the houses, thinking of all the families cozy inside, sitting in warm rooms eating and talking and watching TV. The Kid liked doing that too, going into his parents' house and sitting in their living room reading a history book. His father would have come home from his warehouse job and would be watching TV or talking with Celeste. His mother would be in the kitchen, making dinner. The Kid was grateful to be there.

Not that he ate the dinner his mother served. Her cooking was vile. Because of her, the Kid had a lifelong dislike of Mexican food. Even in the summer, when the barrio was full of people cooking carnitas outdoors, the Kid couldn't join in. He knew the food was excellent, but the smell was so close to the smell of his mother's cooking that his brain couldn't talk his stomach into it. He liked the feel of all the people hanging around outside, cooking and drinking beer. But he wouldn't eat the food, and he wasn't old enough to drink.

From the age of thirteen, the Kid did his own cooking. When he'd complained about his mother's cooking, she'd said, "If you don't like it, don't eat it. Cook your own dinner." She didn't mean it, but the Kid took her at her word. He went to the library and got some books on cooking. His mother didn't have much of the equipment mentioned in the books, and there were many ingredients he'd never heard of. It didn't matter. He made do with what he had. When a recipe included ingredients he wasn't familiar with, he'd go to the store and ask about them. It wasn't long until he could quickly figure whether an ingredient was essential or just a garnish.

His mother didn't like her position as family cook being challenged, but there wasn't much she could do about it. Her husband and daughter both preferred the Kid's cooking to hers. He would bake or grill fish, stir-fry vegetables and meat, cook pasta, bake bread, and marinate pork, lamb, or chicken. He liked cooking for his parents and sister, even though he didn't like them much. He loved being able to do something well, to produce something that people appreciated and that made them feel good. For the rest of his life, the Kid would hate restaurants that served uniform, generic food, prefrozen and heated up by rote, like items being assembled on a factory conveyor belt. What the Kid liked about cooking was the care that went into it. He said that when you were making a meal, you should always be thinking of the people who would eat it. "Then you'll do it good," he said. "You'll do it nice."

When he grew up, the Kid should have been a chef somewhere. But that couldn't happen, because he'd have had to go to a college, a cooking school, and that was something that couldn't happen for him. That wasn't who he was. And he could never have tolerated being the cook in some joint where you just take something from the fridge and put it in the microwave.

THREE

When people say that the Kid couldn't fight unless he had a weapon, they're mostly right. It's true that he didn't like to use his fists. He never grew to be more than five feet six, and he never weighed more than a hundred and twenty. Most men were stronger than him, and he knew it. He'd probably never have learned anything about fistfighting if his first girlfriend hadn't been a boxer.

The Kid was fifteen and spent most of his evenings hanging out. After cooking dinner for his family, he'd wander across the barrio to the house of a guy named Tommy, who was twenty-one. Tommy's place was a gathering point for kids. His door was always open, and when you walked into his living room it was like walking into a bar or café. There was no carpet on the concrete floor, but there were three couches and some chairs. Tommy had gotten one of the couches from his mother and the other two from thrift stores. He worked in a copy shop, and aside from that he just hung out full-time. On any evening of the week, there would be anywhere from twenty to thirty kids there, aged from about fourteen to twenty-two. The room always smelled of weed. On weekends there were parties, and as many as a hundred people might be there before the cops showed up to send everybody home and bust whoever they could for drugs or curfew violation.

Lisa hung out there a couple nights a week, the nights when she wasn't training. She was fifteen, and she spent most of her nights at the boxing club. She hadn't had a fight yet, because there wasn't an abundance of teenage female boxers to choose an opponent from. But now they had found someone for her, and she was about to make her debut.

She was heavyset, but not fat, with the big hair, heavy makeup, and big earrings favored by cholas. Some of the guys were attracted to her, and others thought she was gross. But nobody came on to her except for some of the older guys. She had a mouth, and the younger guys were afraid of her.

The Kid liked her, but he didn't know what to do about it. He never got to talk to her much when they were at Tommy's. She talked a lot, and the Kid hardly talked at all. He wasn't shy, he just couldn't think of things to say in a big group. He would sit there and look at Lisa and smile at her and not say anything. When he got home he would lie in bed and think about her, imagine kissing her and touching her, and he'd come in his hand. He never imagined fucking her, because he couldn't imagine fucking, couldn't imagine what it would feel like.

One night at Tommy's, the Kid said, "Hey, Lisa."

"Yeah, what?" The place was busy. She was sitting on the floor, drinking soda and talking to a couple of girls.

"Can I talk to you for a minute?"

"Yeah," she said, but she didn't move from her position on the floor. Her friends grinned at each other, seeing what was up.

"Can you come outside for a minute?" the Kid asked her.

"Yeah, I guess." As she stood up, she looked at her friends and bugged her eyes, and they laughed. The Kid went outside and stood in the front yard. Lisa followed, but she took her time.

"So. What can I do for you?" she said.

The Kid felt his ass contract, and he almost told her to forget it. But it had taken so long for him to screw up enough courage to approach her, he didn't think he'd be able to manage it a second time. It would have to be now. So he did something that nearly always worked for him when he was scared: he pretended that he was outside of his body, standing behind himself like he was somebody else, watching himself do it.

"Nothing much," he said. "I just wanted to ask you if you want to hang out with me sometime."

"We already do. We hang out here."

"I mean, just with me. It's okay if you don't want to."

"That's okay. I want to."

"When?"

"How about tomorrow night?"

Tomorrow was a Friday, and the Kid had some business to take care of. "Gotta work tomorrow," he said. "How about Saturday?"

"I'm fighting Saturday night. My first one. You want to come see it? We can go out after."

"Yeah, that's cool."

She told him the time and place. Then she motioned towards the house. "You going back in?"

"Nah. I gotta be somewhere." He didn't have to be anywhere, but he couldn't handle the anticlimax of going back in the house and just hanging out. Maybe Lisa would change her mind if she had to look at him that long.

"Okay, Saturday," she said. Then she went inside.

The Kid walked home, across the barrio, past the Circle Ks with the vatos standing around outside, past the bars and the taco stands under the streetlights and sky. A big muscle car crawled along the street and pulled up behind the Kid. He looked over his shoulder, saw the guys in the car and stopped walking. The car drove away.

When the Kid arrived home, his father was asleep on the living room couch and his mother and sister were watching TV. They didn't say anything to the Kid, and he didn't say anything to them. He went to his room and lay on the bed and thought about Lisa while he jacked off. After he came, he was still thinking about her, and he thought about her for a long time.

— * —

The gym was called Rodriguez Brothers Boxing Club. There was a taco stand outside. A guy cooking beef and chicken over mesquite. The Kid asked him how he did it, and the guy showed him. Then the guy asked the Kid if he wanted one.

"I don't like tacos much," the Kid said.

"Where did you eat them?"

"Just at home. My mom's. They suck."

"Okay," the guy said. "I'm gonna make you one. If you don't like it, you don't pay. All right?"

The Kid agreed. The guy asked if he wanted beef or chicken, and he chose beef. As he watched the guy cook, he asked him, "Do you do this every day?"

"Every day except Sunday. Sunday is for family and God. I only started about a month ago."

"Do you like it?"

"Yeah, it's cool. It's not easy, starting your own business. But it's cool not having some jerkoff telling me what to do."

The Kid imagined himself doing this, cooking his food and selling it to people passing by.

The vendor gave him the taco. He ate it, and it was good. He paid for it, and told the guy he'd get another one after the fights.

The gym was almost full. It wasn't the type of crowd he'd expected to see at a boxing show—mostly families with small children, which gave the place the atmosphere of a fair. They sat in rows of folding chairs around the full-size ring at the center of the gym. All the punching bags had been taken down and put away to make room. Against a wall, a candle burned in front of a shrine to the Virgin of Guadalupe. A little girl played with a plaid-suited toddler who kept trying to climb the steps to the ring. At the back of the room, a teenage boy with dark brown skin and long black hair, baseball cap on backwards, hands wrapped in grimy bandages, shadowboxed with ferocious quickness as his coach looked on, circling and instructing him.

The Kid found a seat. It was near the back, but the place was so small that he still had a good view of the ring. He got a program. Lisa's fight was third on the bill. The first fight was between two very small boys who didn't look like they could be older than ten. One of them stood near the Kid's seat as his coach put the gloves on him. It felt strange to the Kid to watch the boy stretching and warming up like a pro as he talked to his coach in a high, unbroken voice. The gloves were as big as his head.

The fight was comical. The families and friends of the boys screamed support and abuse as if they were ringside at a world title fight, while the boys nervously jabbed at each other. The fight went three rounds, each round just a minute long. When the final bell rang, the Kid wasn't able to pick a winner, but the judges managed to.

The second fight was better, but the Kid didn't pay much attention to it. He'd noticed Lisa waiting near the ring.

Her hair was tied in a ponytail and pulled through the back of her headguard. There were gloves on her hands, and she wore boxing shorts, shoes and a tank top. The Kid looked at her bare arms and shoulders, her tight muscles, the black cotton stretched across her big tits.

Lisa got in the ring, and so did her opponent, who looked to be at least twenty pounds heavier. She had the look of a mean bull dyke, and her build seemed better suited to sumo wrestling than boxing. She reminded the Kid of Bull Marie from the *Love and Rockets* comic books he read sometimes.

"Next up is a featherweight contest," announced the emcee. "Between, on my right, in the red corner, representing the Rodriguez Boxing Club, Li-sa Sal-cido . . ." A bunch of guys, Lisa's clubmates, cheered louder than the rest. She stepped out of the corner and waved to them. She didn't look at the Kid.

". . . And, in the blue corner, from the Albuquerque Sporting Club, Chris-tina Ber-nal."

Christina saluted the crowd as Lisa had. Then the referee called them to ring center for their instructions. The girls listened to him, then touched gloves and went back to their corners. Lisa's coach said something to her as he put in her mouthpiece.

The bell rang.

The girls went straight for each other. You wouldn't have known that either of them had ever had a boxing lesson—they just ran to the middle of the ring and started wailing on each other. Neither would back off. Neither threw a single body punch. They just windmilled punches to the head. Lisa looked puny compared with Christina, but neither of them was about to give. When the bell rang to end the round, they grinned insolently at each other and walked to their corners.

In the second round, Christina got on top and looked set to steamroll Lisa. Her bulk was starting to make a difference, and Lisa couldn't hold her ground. But Lisa backed off and started to box, scoring with an accurate jab and banging hooks to Christina's head. Christina just kept swinging. The round was even.

In her corner, Lisa seemed calm. So did Christina, but she was breathing hard. At the start of the third and last round, Lisa almost skipped from her stool. Christina pulled herself from hers.

The last round was a replay of the first. The girls ignored defense and just stood there and battered each other. The crowd went apeshit. Christina was still as aggressive, but she seemed exhausted. Lisa raised her pace as Christina slackened hers. When the final bell rang, the girls ignored it and kept fighting. The referee pushed them apart and ordered them to their corners.

The Kid watched as Lisa spat her mouthpiece into her coach's hand. The coach removed her headguard and gloves. Her hands were taped and bandaged. She ran a hand through her hair, which was slick with sweat. She looked at the Kid and smiled.

The fighters were called to ring center for the announcement of the decision. It was obvious that both girls thought they'd won. The decision went to Lisa. When the referee raised her hand, she whooped and punched the air with her other hand. Christina shook her head but slapped Lisa on the back.

Lisa was given a trophy, a plastic statue of a boxer painted gold. When she got out of the ring, some of the guys from the boxing club were waiting to congratulate her. The Kid waited. When Lisa was walking to the dressing room, he went up to her and said, "Hey."

"Hey."

"Good fight."

"Thanks. My coach is mad at me because I got too excited and just brawled."

"Everybody else liked it. Hey, are you gonna stay for the rest of the show or do you want to go do something?"

"We can go," she said. "Just wait while I get changed."

"Okay. I'll be outside."

The Kid went out to the taco stand and asked the vendor to make a couple. When Lisa came out of the gym, he handed her a taco and a can of Coke.

"Thanks," she said. She was dressed more casually than usual: jeans, a hooded sweatshirt, a denim jacket. Her hair was pulled into a bun. No earrings or makeup. She was a little bit swollen around the eyes, and her lips were puffy. The Kid still thought she was beautiful.

"So what do you feel like doing?" he asked her.

"I don't care. But I need to go home and take a shower. I feel gross. They don't have a shower in the gym."

"You look awesome."

She laughed. "And I have to tell my mom and dad I won. They don't like me fighting. They were too worried to come."

She lived a couple of miles from the gym. They walked. She had her gym bag over her shoulder, and she carried her trophy in her hand. The Kid asked if she wanted him to carry something, but she said no.

"So what made you want to be a boxer?" the Kid asked her.

"Don't know. I just like it. My dad watches the fights on TV, and I always get excited."

"Do you get scared of getting hurt?"

"Nah. It doesn't hurt. People think getting punched will hurt, but it doesn't. You ever had a filling in one of your teeth?"

"Yeah."

"And you feel the drill on your tooth, but it doesn't hurt? Being punched in a fight's like that. You feel it hit you, but it doesn't hurt."

"Are you going to keep on doing it?"

"Oh, yeah. You know, they're talking about having women boxers at the Olympic Games soon."

"Would you like to be a pro fighter?"

"Sure. But that don't look like it's happening for women like it does for men. There are some women pros, but not many. It's not a career. I'm gonna go to school."

"What kind of job do you want?"

"A probation officer."

"Yeah?"

"Yeah. And from what people say about you, you could be one of my guys."

"What do people say about me?"

"That you're nuts. You're a psycho."

"Who says that?"

"A lot of people."

"You know anybody who ever saw me do anything?"

"No."

"I'll bet the people who say things like that don't even know me."

"Maybe."

They walked in silence for a moment. Then she asked him, "What do you want to do when you finish school?"

"I don't know yet."

"Want to go to college?"

"I guess. I don't know."

"What do you think you might want to do?"

"I don't know." Searching for something, he said, "Be a chef, maybe."

"Can you cook?"

"Yeah. My mom don't cook no more. I do it."

"Cool. Where did you learn to do it? Did your mom show you?"

"No. I got it from books."

"You like to read?"

"Yeah. Do you?"

"Not much. I just read for school."

When they reached her house, the Kid said, "I know it's dumb, but I'm shy about meeting your mom and dad. Not really . . . Meeting them's okay. I'm just nervous about hanging out with them while you take a shower."

"It'd be okay. They're pretty cool. But it's okay if you don't want to. But if I have to look like this, we can't go anywhere people can see me."

"If you feel like just keeping on walking, that's cool with me."

She laughed. "You're fucking weird . . . Okay, we can do that."

Her living room reminded him of his own, but her parents didn't remind him of his. They asked her in detail about the fight, and pretended to be thrilled that she'd won even though the truth was that they were just glad she wasn't hurt. She introduced the Kid, and they gave him a polite interrogation, which he handled by lying wherever possible and keeping his answers general when he thought Lisa might know if he lied.

"We're gonna take a walk," Lisa told her parents.

"To where?" asked her father, bemused. He looked at the Kid. "She never walks anywhere! Did she get hit in the head too many times tonight?"

"Well, it's late. I don't have time to get ready. And I'm not going to a café or anything looking like this," said Lisa.

"When'll you be back?" her mother asked.

"Couple hours, probably," she said.

— * —

The alley wasn't as dark as they'd have liked, but they were pressed so far into a doorway that you'd have had to walk past and look to see them. Lisa's hair had pulled out of its bun. She was sucking the Kid's tongue deep into her mouth. The Kid was feeling her tits through her sweatshirt. She took his hands in hers and moved them under her shirt. His hands were cold and she gasped at the shock.

"You okay?" he said.

"Yeah. Just cold. See how you like it." She shoved a hand down into his pants and he laughed and groaned at the same time.

He kept feeling her tits as she unzipped his pants and began stroking his cock. When he was close, she took a step back, looked at him and went down on her knees. She rubbed her face against his cock, then sucked on it.

He came in her mouth.

She swallowed, hard, then licked what was left of it from his cock. "Mmmm."

He didn't do anything to make her come. He didn't know how. They walked back to her house, holding hands. He didn't go in. They kissed for a few minutes more. He could taste himself in her mouth. She said she'd call him.

— * —

She called him and told him that her parents were going to Albuquerque on Monday night and wouldn't be coming back until late. Did he want to come over? He said he'd see her then.

He had something else to think about first. He had bought some speed from a dealer at an unusually low price, and made a serious profit when he sold it. Then he'd found out why it was so cheap, when some of his customers came to him and said the stuff must be Alka-Seltzer or something, that it had no effect. He'd called the guy he'd bought it from and said he wanted his money back. The guy kept saying okay, but he never paid up.

On Sunday night, the Kid went to the guy's home. He lived in a shared apartment on Don Cubero Alley, just off Cerrillos Road. It was snowing, and the Kid sat in the Aztec Café and drank a hot cider before making his visit. When he'd finished his cider, he left the Aztec and walked along Cerrillos. He liked the dark and the streetlights and the wind blowing the snow and nobody else around. Sometimes it felt as though he liked everything. He walked up Don Cubero and found the apartment. He knocked, and the guy came to the door.

His name was Jeff. He was white, around twenty-five, and always seemed to be about to laugh when he dealt with the Kid.

"Oh, hey," he said, when he saw the Kid. "Come on in."

"No, thanks," the Kid said. "I don't have time. I just came to tell you not to worry about giving me the money back. Shit happens."

"For real?"

"Yeah," the Kid said. He pulled the knife out of his pocket and drew it across Jeff's face, left and right, ripping deep. The edge of the blade was serrated so that it would leave a permanent mark wherever it cut.

"Ohshitshitshitshitohgod—" Jeff's face opened up, came apart, his mouth got huge, wide, and he started to move without knowing whether he was trying to back away or turn and run or defend himself, while the Kid just stood there holding the knife.

His roommate came out of the living room. "Oh, fuck. I'm calling the cops."

"You do that, homes," the Kid said. "If you want what he just got. You call the cops." Then he looked at Jeff. "And if you say a word to them, I'll come back and cut your fucking ears off." He wiped the blade on Jeff's shirt and walked away.

"Oh, man," said Jeff's roommate. "Oh, man. He cut you. He really cut you."

"Lock the fucking door in case he comes back," Jeff bawled. His roommate went to the door. Just before he closed it, he saw the Kid walking away from the apartment, walking against the snow.

— * —

On Monday evening, the Kid went to Lisa's house. It was around seven. He knocked on the door. She opened it, and she was dressed the way she usually was, her make-up carefully applied. "Come on in."

They went straight to her bedroom. She put a CD in her stereo and hit the play button. This was around the time that Mexicans were getting out of the habit of calling blacks gringos and starting to identify with rap, so the album was *The Chronic*. "You like this?" she asked the Kid.

"Yeah." He took off his shoes and they lay on the bed.

Bow-wow-wow, yippee-o, yippee-ay, Doggy Dogg's in the muthafuckin' house . . .

"Did you miss me?" she said.

"Yeah." The Kid wanted to kiss her, but he didn't know how to start, didn't know how long they had to talk before they could do anything else.

Lisa put him out of his misery. She snuggled up to him and kissed him on the mouth. They kissed for a while, and the Kid was afraid he was going to come in his pants. He didn't last much longer. They took their clothes off, and when the Kid saw Lisa's naked body, the precome was dripping from his cock. He was lying on his back. As soon as she touched him, he spurted into her hand.

"Sorry," he said.

"Don't be," she said. "I like it." She looked into his face as she rubbed his come into her tits. He was hard again in minutes. They made out for a while, then Lisa said, "You want to do me?"

"Yeah." The Kid wasn't sure. He looked at the size of his cock and couldn't imagine how it would fit into her. He was afraid it would hurt him or her.

She made to straddle him. The Kid said, "We need to get a rubber or something . . . "

"I'm on the pill."

"You been with many guys?"

"Not many. You think I'm a ho or something?"

"I just asked."

"You're the fifth. I take the pill for heavy periods."

"Oh."

"How about you?"

"Do I take the pill?"

"Am I your first?"

"No." He never knew if she believed him.

His cock got soft as she tried to pull it inside her. "What's wrong?" she asked.

"I don't know."

She sucked on his cock for a little while. It got hard again, but softened when she tried to fuck him. "You nervous?" she asked.

"Yeah." He was looking at his soft cock, not at her.

"It's okay," she said. "C'mere." She put her arms around him and guided his face to her tits. He kissed the left one. "Suck it," she said. He did, and she stroked his hair and bit his ear, moaning a little. She lay back and moved his head down her body, letting him lick her navel, then pushed him down farther until he was licking at her cunt.

He was afraid he wouldn't like the taste, but he did. He pushed his tongue inside her and she came right away, grinding against his face so hard it hurt his nose. When she was quiet again, she pulled him up on top of her and kissed him. His cock was very hard, and she got it into her wetness just by pressing against him. He let out a small whimper that somehow seemed very loud, and clung to her.

— * —

The Kid and Lisa were together a lot in the next few weeks. They'd go see movies, sit around coffeehouses or hang out at Tommy's place. The Kid began to think of her as his girlfriend, though they never talked about it that way.

One night they were at Tommy's. A lot of people were smoking, and the Kid didn't smoke. Neither did Lisa. They decided to go outside.

There was nobody in the yard but them. The Kid put an arm around Lisa and kissed her. She kissed him back, opening her mouth and reaching for his tongue with hers. But then she stepped away from him.

"I don't want to do this anymore," she said.

The Kid didn't know why, and he didn't ask. He was too frightened. "Okay," he said.

"Sorry," she said.

"It's okay."
"I'm going back inside."
"Okay. See you later."

— * —

He did see her, usually at Tommy's, sometimes around town. She always said hello, but that was it. Pretty soon, the Kid stopped going to Tommy's.

Something had changed in him. I don't know what it was, because the Kid never knew what it was, and he wasn't someone who'd have tried to figure it out. It had something to do with Lisa, but it wasn't all about her. The Kid started going to see boxing shows, and he went to a gym and sparred a little, but he wasn't that good at it and he never fought a competition. It was just because Lisa had done it. Then that got old for him and he pretty much forgot about her, except for the sex. But something had still changed. He had never really minded the way his life was, and now he did.

His sister had a recording of Abba's greatest hits, and would play it constantly. The song "Chiquitita" was on it. When the Kid heard it coming from her room, it always conjured a picture in him of a young blonde woman wearing a woolen hat. Snow behind her. There was no reference to such an image in the song, so he probably got it from hearing that Abba was Swiss or Swedish—he was never sure which, and he wouldn't have known the difference anyway.

That winter, inside his head, he kept singing that song to himself. Or rather, the fragments of it that he knew. All the guys he knew thought Abba was pathetic, music for little girls and gay men, but he thought the song was beautiful. "Chiquitita, tell me what's wrong/ You're enchained by your own sorrow/In your eyes there is no hope for tomorrow/. . . Chiquitita, tell me the truth/I'm a shoulder you can cry on/Your best friend, and the one you must rely on." That gorgeous guitar, and the melody so sad. And her voice so caring, so concerned. The Kid wanted her to care for him.

It mattered to him now that his family didn't. For the first time, he began reading fiction, the stories in his sister's teen magazines, stories of true love in which lonely, hurt people always ended up being saved.

Nobody saved the Kid. But nothing could stop him from dreaming about it. He started cutting school, and, so he wouldn't meet anybody who knew him and might tell his parents, he'd walk out of the barrio and into the suburbs. The trees would be huge and bare of leaves and coated with frost. He'd trudge along, curled up inside his head, singing "Chiquitita" to himself. He'd imagine the blonde woman in the snow was singing for him, because she loved him and couldn't stand to see him hurting so much. She was telling him that he had to trust her, that she was on his side and wanted to be with him, no matter what anybody else thought or said.

He'd sometimes go into a store or café to get something to eat, and sometimes the store clerk or waiter would ask if he shouldn't be at school. At fifteen, he looked younger. No, he'd say, he was doing some kind of project. One time, he was crossing the Plaza in the center of Santa Fe, and a landscaping crew was working on the gardens. One of them, a guy in his twenties or thirties, looked at him and said, "You cutting school?"

"No. I've got the day off."

"So how come you've got a bag with your school books?"

"This ain't my school bag. There's no books in it."

"Let me see."

"It's none of your business."

"Little fuck!" The guy walked towards the Kid, dropping the rake he'd been using. The Kid turned and ran, sprinting hard, swinging his arms. When he stopped and looked back, he saw that the man hadn't come after him. He was talking to one of his workmates. If it hadn't been in the middle of the day, in front of witnesses, the man would probably be dead.

FOUR

The Kid found some advantages in his parents not caring about him. It meant he could do anything he wanted. They would only have cared about his cutting school because it might have gotten them in trouble. The Kid never knew if they realized that he was dealing drugs. But they must have known he was doing something illegal, because he didn't have a job and he had more money than most of the kids his age who had jobs. But they just told him, over and over, that if he ever brought the cops to their door he would never be allowed back in their house.

When he was sixteen, he paid twelve hundred dollars for a clunking old 1977 Chevy Impala. It looked ready for the scrap yard, but it had a very good engine, and girls liked it. He'd drive around Santa Fe in the evenings, sometimes parking on one of the streets off the Plaza, walking up to the Plaza and hanging out there with his friends, making the rich kids nervous. In Santa Fe, the main activity for kids at night is driving around trying to find a party. On weekend nights, he'd often drive to Albuquerque, go to an all ages show, or just cruise around.

The Kid was making better and better connections in the drug industry. He was becoming known in places that he'd never even heard of, places South of the Border. The narcos knew of him as somebody who would be big in the life, a child who terrified adults.

Then he got busted.

— * —

I don't know what it was for; there are so many stories about it. But it can't have been very serious, because he was only sentenced to a year inside.

His first day inside felt like his first day at school, and he handled it the same way. He kept quiet and did as he was told. He soon stopped being nervous. Many of the boys he was locked up with had killed people, but they didn't seem very different than most of the people on the outside. His father had said, "I hope you get raped up the ass every day," but nothing like that happened. The Kid took a reputation inside with him, and nobody wanted to try to turn him into their bitch. People made passes at him, but nobody forced it when he said no.

He knew he was lucky. There was a boy there who didn't come in with a reputation, but came in with the same slight build and quiet manner as the Kid. The boy had almost immediately become the bitch of a bigger, tougher boy, who made him sleep under his bunk and lent him out to other people. He'd tell his friends, "Yeah, you can borrow him." The boy would say nothing, just go with his master's friend, who would fuck him in the ass or the mouth or both. Then he'd come back, still saying nothing, and curl up under the bed.

The Kid masturbated a lot. Even before being locked up, when he was getting laid plenty, he had been in the habit of jacking off at least twice a day, when he woke up in the morning and last thing at night. In confinement, with no girls around, the frequency increased. But he never considered guys. This might have been because he knew he was just going to be there for a year. He wondered if it might be different if he was there for a long time, if he would become attracted to men through loneliness and conditioning.

He didn't find it to be any lonelier in there than on the outside. His family never visited him or wrote to him, but that didn't feel like anything new. The violence around him didn't bother him much. The worst thing about incarceration was other people's bodies, having to share cells and showers and toilets. The smell of someone else's breath, piss, shit, semen. And the other, unidentifiable smells that bodies produce. Waiting to piss or shit because someone else has just taken a shit in the toilet you have to use. The Kid hated the sight of other guys spitting out toothpaste, washing their asses.

But he made some friends and he learned a lot. He didn't like being told what to do by the guards, but other than that it wasn't too bad. He didn't talk back, and most of the guards seemed to like him.

Except for one, whose name was Voas. He was a large, hairy, stupid-looking man of forty who nonetheless seemed to suffer from

Little Man's Syndrome. He'd been a promising football player in college, and had thought he was going somewhere with that. But he was too cowardly for the big leagues, and he quit the game after being knocked unconscious while trying to run away from another player. He didn't finish college, and he didn't do much of anything else. He'd taken the job as a guard because he wanted to be a tough guy, the kind of guard you see in movies like *Cool Hand Luke*. The way he talked to his friends, it sounded as though he was the warden at Sing Sing, rather than a turnkey at a boys' farm. It burned his ass that none of the inmates respected him, even with his size and bullying manner. The other guards commanded more respect without even trying, and they all thought Voas was an asshole. To impress his peers, he tried harder and harder to be Charles Bronson, and the inmates laughed at him more and more.

He couldn't stand the Kid. It wasn't anything the Kid said—most of the other inmates were mouthier—it was the contemptuous way the Kid looked at him. The others would sometimes be provoked by Voas's antics, but the Kid just seemed amused.

Voas kept telling the Kid he'd better watch it with the "dumb insolence," but the Kid never did anything he could write him up for. A lot of drugs were finding their way into the institution, and Voas was sure that the Kid had something to do with it, though there was no way he could prove anything. But he never stopped looking for a way to hurt the Kid. And eventually he found it.

The institution had a visiting artist, who came once a week to work with inmates who wanted to learn to draw or write. Her name was Chrissie. Although she was white, she was interested in panos, an art form created by Latino prisoners. Panos are drawn on handkerchiefs with pens, and are usually created as gifts for family and friends on the outside. The Kid had never seen any art that he thought had anything to do with him, but panos contained nothing but the images of the barrio—the two most common, Chrissie told her students, were the Virgin of Guadalupe, and the peacock, which symbolized pride and the lowrider. Panos would often contain both images. The drawings were dense, very detailed, and often used to convey messages that would be censored if written in letters.

Chrissie was a good teacher. She'd come from white trash, and she didn't talk down to the boys or go touchy-feely on them. She asked about their lives, not like a sociologist but like a neighbor, and they talked to her. Before long, she had a number of boys working on panos. She was well connected on the Santa Fe art scene, and she hustled a gallery owner into agreeing to let her curate an exhibition of panos there. She asked her students if they wanted to contribute, and they all said yes. Especially the Kid. He wasn't very good at drawing, but he loved doing panos, and Chrissie thought there was an unusual wit to his drawing, crude as it was. His panos had the usual images, but also food, snow, girls, empty streets. He knew he wasn't technically great, but he drew every day. He told Chrissie, "If I do a lot of panos, they probably won't all suck."

Shortly before Chrissie was due to come and pick up all the panos for the exhibition, Voas accused the Kid of involvement in the inmates' drug trade. The Kid just shrugged and said he had nothing to do with it and didn't know anything about it. Voas told him his cell would have to be searched.

"What for? What makes you think I did anything?"

Voas shoved the Kid. "And what makes you think I have to explain anything to you, you little prick?"

The Kid didn't answer. He just gave Voas that condescending look.

The Kid was taken out of his cell while it was searched. When he was brought back to it, he asked, straight-faced, if anything had been found. He'd been a little worried that Voas might plant something. "No," Voas said. "But that doesn't mean you're not doing it. It just means we're not looking in the right places."

The Kid said nothing.

The next day, the Kid drew two panos. When he went to put them with all the others he'd done, he found that they were gone.

"I didn't see any handkerchiefs," Voas said.

"You're a fucking liar."

"Watch it . . ."

"You watch it. You fucking stole my panos." The Kid felt his eyes get wet. He fought it and won.

Voas looked at the guard who was with him. "Looks like we got a crybaby here," he said. He wanted the other guard to laugh, but he didn't even smile.

"What's your problem?" the Kid said. "Are you on the rag?"

Voas looked at him.

"Your boyfriend keep coming in your mouth? Is that it?" the Kid said.

"Don't push your luck, boy."

"I'm not pushing anything. I want my panos back."

"Well, you better find out where they are," Voas said, and smiled.

"I'll tell you something. If I don't get my panos back, I'm going to cut your fucking throat."

Voas laughed, and spread his arms. "Whenever you're ready. Come on."

The Kid didn't make any move, but the other guard got in between them. "Come on, chill out," he told Voas.

"I'm not doing anything. He threatened me."

"That's right," said the Kid. "I ain't gonna do nothing to you now. I can't. But when I get out of here I'm gonna find out where you live, and you're gonna be dead."

Voas turned to the other guard. "You heard that, right? You heard him say that?"

The guard nodded. "Yeah, I heard it. Come on, he's upset. He's lost his drawings . . ."

Voas wrote the Kid up anyway.

The Kid had been sentenced to a year. His good behavior would have gotten him out in a lot less time than that. But with the write-up for threatening a guard, he lost any chance of that and would have to serve the entire sentence.

He told Chrissie what had happened. She was outraged, but there was nothing she could do about it. Even some of the other guards were pissed at Voas. A couple of them asked him if he really had taken the Kid's panos. He denied it, but nobody believed him. The Kid and his cellmate were friends, and, even if they hadn't been, the cellmate would have been too scared of the Kid to do something like that to him. And, even if he had, where would he have been able to dispose of the panos? No, there was no doubt in anybody's mind that it was Voas.

The inmates expected Voas to get shanked before long. So did many of the guards, and not all of them minded. It didn't happen. A couple of days after the incident, the Kid was treating Voas just as he had before, without hostility, but with the air of someone humoring a backward child. Voas was now watching his back, thinking the Kid was trying to lull him into a false sense of security. He would have liked to take things even further with the Kid, set him up for something, but he was afraid of the reaction of his colleagues. One of them had told him to his face that he was a weasel, and he could see that the others felt the same way, though they didn't say anything. Some of the guards were treating the Kid with more warmth than they treated Voas.

The Kid's cellmate, Armando, asked him if he was going to do anything to Voas.

"I already have," the Kid said.

"What?"

"He shits his pants every time he comes near me. If I reach my hand behind my back, he jumps. Every day, he's waiting for it."

"He gonna get it?"

"I ain't gonna give him any way to keep me in here any longer than they can already. Fuck that. Fuck him. There's always outside."

But the Kid knew that Voas had won. Because, though he wasn't sure why, the Kid didn't want to draw panos anymore.

FIVE

The year ran out, and the Kid was released. Some of the friends he'd made would soon be getting out too, and they gave the Kid phone numbers where they could be reached.

It was a spring morning when they let him out. He could have taken the bus, but he wanted to walk. It took him four hours to walk into town, but he wouldn't have minded if it had been even longer. He walked along the edge of the highway, and every now and then someone would pull over and offer him a ride. He always politely said no, he wanted to walk. He could tell that they thought he was crazy, but it didn't bother him. And it didn't occur to him to suggest that they try being locked up for a year.

The sky was a cool blue, and a light wind was blowing. The Kid walked, live desert on either side of the highway. He came to a convenience store, went in and got some nachos and a can of Dr Pepper. He sat on a low wall outside and ate. Normally he'd have hated the food, the synthetic, cheese-flavored goo that covered the chips. But, after a year of Department of Corrections cuisine, it felt like nothing had ever tasted so good. He swallowed each mouthful with a swig of Dr Pepper, holding it in his mouth until the food became a sweet pulp.

When he'd finished eating, he wiped his sticky fingers with a paper napkin. It didn't get them clean, so he threw the empty can and nachos container in the trash, then went back inside the store and asked the clerk if they had a restroom. She was in her fifties, white, unfriendly. The Kid wondered if she was like that with everybody, or if she somehow knew where he'd been. She crabbily told him where the restroom was. He went in and washed his hands at the sink. The restroom stank, but the stink felt different from the stink in the institution. This place had pubic hairs stuck to the toilet, shit stains in the bowl, splashes of piss on the floor. But it didn't stink of the same people doing the same piss and shit every day. This place had the stink of people who just came through, pissed and shat, and never came back. And that was what the Kid wanted.

He left the restroom, got another Dr Pepper from the fridge and took it to the counter. The clerk didn't look at him as he paid for it. There was something about her sullenness that depressed the Kid. He hadn't done anything to her. Why not be nice to people if they hadn't done anything to you? Outside the store, he opened the can and chugged the soda, then threw the can in the trash. He started to feel better. For the past year, if he'd met a mean, unfriendly person, he couldn't get away from them. Now, with this woman and anybody else, all he had to do was walk.

It was the middle of the afternoon when he got into town. It was just as it had been. He wandered around the Plaza for a while, enjoying the sky and the cars and the buildings. Then he walked to the barrio. He wondered if he would run into anybody he knew, but he didn't. He came to his parents' house and knocked on the door.

His mother opened it.

"Hi," he said.

She just looked at him.

"I wrote to tell you I was getting out today," he said. "Did you get the letter?"

"Yeah."

The Kid stepped forward, making to go inside. But his mother didn't move away from the door.

"You can't come in now," she said.

"Why not?"

"Your dad said. You'll have to wait till he gets home from work."

"Can I come in and wait?"

"No. He said no."

They stood there and looked at each other.

"Okay," the Kid said. "I'll come back later."

His mother didn't say anything. She stood there and watched him walk away. Then she closed the door.

The Kid went back to walking. He walked out of the barrio, over to Guadalupe, walked along Guadalupe to Aztec Street and went into the Aztec Café. It was the scummiest coffeehouse in town, and the

Kid had missed going there. He always looked strange there because he didn't have any tattoos or piercings.

The place hadn't changed. It was in two sections, one for smoking and the other not. The smoking section was larger, and was always busy. The Kid got a hot cider and sat in the nonsmoking section. He wished he had something to read. He'd expected to sit in the café and feel amazed that he was free again, but he didn't feel that way at all. Already it felt like his incarceration had happened a long time ago, or else had only lasted for a short time, a few days maybe, and now it was over and things were back to normal. He knew that wasn't how it was, but what he knew wasn't the same as what he felt.

He also knew that he should be thinking about what to do next, thinking about what would happen when he spoke to his father. But he didn't feel able to think about anything like that. So he sat there in the café and drank his cider, and then he left and walked all the way back to his parents' house.

It was just after six o'clock when he got there. He knocked on the door. He heard his mother and father talking, then footsteps, then the door opened and his father was standing there looking at him. At first neither of them spoke. Then his father said, "What do you want?"

"I got out today."

"I can see that. So what do you want?"

"I came home. I want to come home."

"This ain't your home."

"Yes it is."

"No it ain't. Not no more."

"But I ain't got nowhere else."

"That's your problem. I told you, you better never bring the cops to my door, and you did. You ain't welcome here."

They were silent for a moment, just looking at each other. The Kid could see that his father wasn't going to change his mind. But, for some reason, he said, "Nobody came to see me."

"Nobody wanted to come see you. You weren't missed."

"Where's my car?" the Kid asked him.

"Parked around the back. Take it."

"Has anybody been using it?"

"No."

The Kid didn't believe him.

"What about my stuff?"

"It's all in your room. Nobody's touched it. Come in and get it."

The Kid followed him into the house. As he walked through the hall he tried to look in the living room door, but his father shoved him from behind, not hard, but firm enough to propel him towards his room. Or the room that had been his.

He pushed the door open, turned on the light, and went in. The room had no dust in it, so his mother must have been cleaning it, but everything seemed to be as he had left it. The bed was made, his clothes hung in the closet, his books were on their shelves, his boom box sat in a corner.

"You got fifteen minutes," said his father. "Pack up and leave. And don't come back."

"I need to get some boxes to put my books in."

"You should have thought of that before. You got fifteen minutes."

"How could I have thought of it before? I didn't know you were gonna kick me out."

"I'm not arguing with you. Fifteen minutes, then you leave or I call the cops. You want to spend your fifteen minutes arguing with me?"

"No. I don't want to argue."

"Then start packing."

The Kid pulled a couple of bags out from under the bed and went through his closet fast, grabbing the clothes he wanted. He knew he wouldn't have time to pack everything, so he only took what he really liked and would definitely wear, shoving each item into the bag as hard as he could, trying to fit in as much as the space would take. He'd filled both bags within ten minutes. His father stood there and watched him. The Kid scanned the bookshelf, which contained about fifty books. He grabbed three or four of them, including his favorites, Howard Zinn's *A People's History of the United States* and James Beard's *American Cookery*. He stuffed them into one of the bags. Then he looked at his father.

"I can go get some boxes right now and take the books."

"No. You got four minutes left."

"Please."

"No. You going to spend your four minutes arguing with me?"

"I just want my books. What're you gonna do with them?"

"Everything you leave will be thrown out or sold tomorrow, Kid. I've had it with you."

The Kid had an impulse to tear the books up one by one, make sure his father couldn't sell them. But he knew there wasn't enough time to do that. And he knew he couldn't have done it anyway.

He opened a drawer and found a set of keys to his car. "Okay," he said to his father. "That's it."

He picked up the bags. He thought about taking the boom box, but it would be hard to carry and he didn't care that much about it anyway. His father followed him outside and they walked to the back of the house, where his car was parked. It was dirty, and the rain had rusted it, but otherwise it looked all right. He put the bags in the trunk. Then he opened the door and got in, got behind the wheel.

The gas gauge said the tank was half-full. The Kid had a feeling that the car wouldn't start. But he stuck the key in and turned it, and it came to life with a quiet rumble. He sat there, letting it warm up.

His father knocked on the window. The Kid rolled it down.

"You don't listen good, so I'm gonna tell you again, just in case. Don't ever come back here, for anything. You hear me?"

The Kid nodded. Then he rolled up the window. He put the car in drive and hit the gas and didn't look in his rearview as he left.

He went a few blocks until he saw a vacant lot. He pulled into it and parked. Then he thought about his books and put his face in his hands and cried.

— * —

The guy's name was Miguel. He was a dealer, like the Kid, but he wasn't into muscle, so the Kid had done a few things for him in the past. He was about five years older than the Kid. He lived in town, just off Guadalupe. The Kid pulled up outside the house, went and knocked on the door. No answer. He was walking back to his car when he saw Miguel walking along the street.

"Jesus motherfuckin' Christ! Hey, man!" Miguel said when he saw the Kid. They shook hands, and Miguel pounded the Kid on the back. "When the fuck did you get out, bro?"

"Today."

"Yeah? For real? Jesus Christ. What you doing?"

"I came to see you. I'm lucky you showed up. I was just about to leave."

"Yeah, I just took a walk. Hey, you hungry?"

"Yeah, kind of."

"Okay, I'm buying. Where you wanna go?"

They went to the Cowgirl Hall of Fame, a bar and restaurant on Guadalupe. It was less than a mile from Miguel's house, so they walked. It was dark and chilly now, but they walked fast and the Kid got a sweat on. They went into the restaurant and sat at a table. The Kid ordered a chicken fried steak and a soda. Miguel got tortilla soup and a beer.

"So what you gonna do now you're a free man?" Miguel said.

"Same as I was doing before, I guess. I got to figure how to get back into it, get something going."

Miguel shook his head. "Things ain't the same, Kid. It's amazing how much can happen in a year, you know? Even I don't sell no more, except for some pot, and that's just to people I know. And a little ecstasy to the rave kids, but that ain't much."

"How come?"

"The bikers have got the market, bro. Especially crystal, which is where the money is."

"What else do they sell?"

"You name it. Mainly crystal, but everything else too. Including pot, but that ain't a big deal to them, so they leave me alone. It don't matter to them if the people do a little selling themselves."

"How did it happen?" the Kid said.

"What?"

"How did they get the market?"

Miguel spread his arms. "I ain't no fucking economist, you know? It's hard to figure, 'cause there ain't been nothing about it in the business section of the *New Mexican*. But from what I can figure, they just moved in on the people. There was a kind of negative advertising war going on for a while. The bikers make their own shit, so they were saying they could sell it cheaper than the product we get from Mexico. The people were saying, yeah, but you get what you pay for, and the quality of the bikers' shit ain't as good. The bikers are big on violence too, and that's what settled it."

"Jesus. It sounds like McDonald's or something. You gonna tell me the narcos are taking that laying down?"

"They don't care, bro. This is Santa Fe. Long as the bikers ain't got 'Burque, nobody gives a rat's ass. When I want shit for my own personal use, I go to 'Burque and get it, just as a protest."

They both laughed. Then the Kid ate in silence for a moment. "You like your steak?" Miguel said.

"Yeah. You should've tasted the shit I had to eat in jail."

"I plan to avoid that experience entirely."

"How you gonna do that?"

"By staying out of the fucking business."

"So what you doing these days?"

Miguel grinned. "You ain't gonna believe me."

"No shit. What's up?"

"I'm working for the paper. The newspaper."

"You're a reporter?"

"Hell, no. I sell advertising."

"You are messing with me."

"Uh-uh."

They sat there and smiled at each other, agape at the craziness of it. Then the Kid said, "How did you get into that?"

"Well, you know I did okay in high school, and I ain't got no record. My Tia Isabella already works there, so she got me in . . . "

"What do you have to do?"

"I call people up and try to talk them into buying advertising space for their business in the paper."

"The way you talk?"

"No, man. Check this out—Hello, Mr. Martin? Hi, my name is Miguel Solano. I'm on the sales team at the *New Mexican*. Has it ever occurred to you to advertise your business to customers who're as intelligent and well informed as you are? I'm talking about the readers of our newspaper, Mr. Martin . . . Fucking rad, huh?"

The Kid couldn't answer. He was laughing too hard.

"Hey," said Miguel. "Now that you're at large, maybe I should call them up and go, All right, motherfucker, buy some advertising or I'll send the Kid to pay you a visit . . . "

It was dark outside when they left the place. "You coming back to the house?" Miguel said.

"Sure," said the Kid. He felt relieved. He had hoped Miguel would invite him, but he wouldn't have been able to ask.

"You staying with your folks?"

"No. They kicked me out."

"Yeah? So where you gonna stay?"

"Don't know yet. I ain't had time to find someplace."

"You got any money?"

"No. But I'll get some."

"How?"

"Don't know yet."

"You want to crash at my house tonight?"

"Is that okay?"

"Hell, yeah. It's your house, okay?"

"Okay. Thanks."

Miguel had a roommate, but he wasn't home. The Kid and Miguel sat in the living room. "I wish I could lend you some money," Miguel said. "I can lend you a little bit, but I ain't got much . . . "

"It's okay," said the Kid.

"The hell it's okay. You need money. You gonna get a job?"

"Maybe. Don't know what I'd do. Who'd hire me?" The Kid shook his head. "I told you. I'm gonna get back in the life."

— * —

People were afraid of Crowley because Crowley wasn't afraid of anything. It wasn't that he was brave; it was that he didn't care what happened to him. He was a serious meth-head, but it wasn't the meth that made him the way he was.

He was in his fifties, and he had been who he was for a long time. When he was eighteen, he joined the Army and trained as a Ranger. He didn't have any desire to be a soldier, he just wanted to get away from his father, who beat the shit out of him almost every day. During his training, a sergeant pissed on him. Crowley just took it. There was a "company dildo" that was used to sodomize recruits as part of hazing. Many people quit. Crowley didn't. He became very skilled at killing. They sent him to Vietnam, and he liked it. He won two Purple Hearts, did a lot of drugs, and lost count of the number of people he killed. He was considered a hero.

Then he got blown up by a grenade. Nobody was quite sure how it had happened. It was rumored that another grunt had made a mistake, had dropped the grenade instead of throwing it, and Crowley had been standing nearby. The blast picked him up and threw him like a stone, but his body remained whole. They sent him home and he spent nine months in the hospital.

When he was released, he wanted to return to Vietnam, but the Army didn't want to send him back there. He was given an honorable discharge. He still needed to fight, to be part of an army, so he joined the peace movement. It was no different than the Army. As a veteran who had turned, he was valuable to them, just as he had been valuable to the Army as a killer. But he was still being used, and he was becoming aware of it. When he was no longer useful, the Army did nothing to help him, and neither did the peace movement.

He hung around Albuquerque, his hometown, but he couldn't make any friends. Everything people cared about seemed stupid to him. He'd be watching TV with other people, and a news item about the war would come on. His companions would remark on how awful it was, then start discussing which party or bar to go to. Crowley only related to two things now: drugs and fucking. He took speed every day and picked up women in bars. One woman he fucked got pregnant and gave birth to a daughter. Crowley hardly ever saw her.

He drifted between Albuquerque and Santa Fe, washed dishes, labored, and learned to work on bikes. He met bikers, and became one. Others joined the gang, stayed some years, left, and moved on, but Crowley never did. He was always there.

Crowley was in Albuquerque doing some business. He got word from Santa Fe that someone was looking for him there, but he wasn't concerned. He was sitting in a biker bar in downtown Albuquerque when the bartender gave him a heads-up. He looked and saw a boy, a skinny little Mexican who looked to be in his late teens, walking around talking to people. He realized that the boy was asking for him, but he just stayed sitting at the bar and didn't say anything. Then he saw the boy walking towards him.

"Hey, excuse me. Are you Mr. Crowley?" the Kid asked him.

"You know I am. Don just pointed me out to you. You want to call him a liar?"

"No. I was just checking."

"You're underage for this place."

"I ain't drinking. I just heard you were in here."

"What do you want?"

"I want to talk to you about something."

"You're already talking to me. What do you want?"

The Kid lowered his voice. "About meth."

"What about it?"

"You're selling it on my old turf in Santa Fe."

Crowley laughed, showing stained teeth. "Your old turf . . . Who the fuck do you think you are?"

"I used to sell, before I got busted a year ago."

"That's very sad. It must have been terrible for you."

"I just got out . . ."

"Congratulations."

"Now everybody's buying from you, and nobody else is selling because they're scared of you."

"So what do you want?"

"I want to sell too."

"You're not real, you're really not real. You think I'm gonna sell to you? What've you got that I need?"

The Kid shook his head. "I don't want you to sell to me. I don't want to work for you. I want to sell for myself. I don't care what you do. You can sell all you want . . ."

"Thank you. I appreciate your generosity."

"I'll get my own stuff to sell. I won't bother you, and you don't bother me. I don't want to get in a war with you. I just want to sell."

Crowley just sat there and laughed, shaking his big shaggy head. "Anything else I can do for you?" he said.

"Yeah. I need some money, till I get set up and start selling. You've been making money off my customers for a year. If I hadn't been gone, they'd have been buying from me and you wouldn't have made the money. So I think you should give me three hundred dollars."

"Only three hundred? Sure you don't want any more?"

The Kid either ignored the sarcasm or didn't get it. "You can give me more if you want, but I'm only asking for three hundred."

Crowley picked up the bottle of Budweiser he was drinking and chugged the last of it. "Okay," he said. "I ain't flashing money around in here. Let's go outside and we'll take care of it." He heaved himself off his bar stool. The Kid followed him outside. People stared at them as they walked towards the door, the Mexican boy with the birdlike frame and big eyes, and the white man with the flabby gut and solid muscles and gray ponytail.

Outside on the street, Crowley said, "Let's go around back."

There was a small alley behind the bar. When they got there, Crowley reached into a pocket of his denim jacket and pulled out his wallet. He opened it and showed it to the Kid. "Look at this," he said, flipping through bills. "Near five hundred right here. You want it?"

"If you want to give it to me, yeah."

"Sure. I'll give it to you." Crowley closed the wallet and used it to slap the Kid across the face, hard and fast, once on each cheek. The Kid took a step back and stood there looking at Crowley. "Now get your fucking beaner ass out of here and don't come back," Crowley said, putting the wallet away. At the same time, the Kid was fumbling inside his jacket. Crowley smiled. "Oh, what's this?"

The Kid pulled the blade out and held it in front of him.

"Gonna cut me?" said Crowley.

"Take your wallet out and give it to me."

"I already gave it to you. You want it again?"

"I'll rip you open."

"Go ahead. What's stopping you?"

The Kid came forward slowly, waving the knife in front of him. Crowley's smile disappeared. He watched the Kid's eyes. The Kid lunged, stabbing at Crowley's chest. Crowley stepped to the side and kicked the Kid's legs from under him. The Kid fell, but held on to the knife. Crowley put a foot on his wrist, pinning his arm to the ground.

"Let go of the knife."

"Blow me, you white trash piece of shit."

With his other foot, Crowley kicked the Kid in the stomach. It hurt more than anything the Kid had ever experienced, like his insides had been torn loose, but it took so much of his breath he couldn't even scream. His hand lost the knife. Crowley took his foot off the Kid's wrist, and the Kid wrapped both arms around his body, crying, waiting for Crowley to kick him again.

Crowley didn't. He picked up the knife. Then he took a handful of the Kid's hair and hauled him to his feet. The Kid's entire body was shaking, and tears were streaming over his face.

"Look at me," Crowley said. The Kid got his eyes in focus and looked into Crowley's face. Crowley pressed the knife against the Kid's throat. "Do you hear me? Are you listening?"

"Yeah," the Kid whimpered.

"If you weren't so young, I'd slice your fucking face off right now. I'll do it anyway if you ever come near me again. Do you hear what I'm saying?"

"Yeah."

Crowley let go of the Kid, who fell to his knees and rolled onto his side. "Take a warning, okay?"

The Kid nodded.

Crowley walked away, went back into the bar.

The Kid wanted to lie there for a long time. He didn't feel like he could stand up. But he was afraid that Crowley might change his mind and come back for him, so he pushed himself to his feet and leaned against the wall. Then, bent almost double, he limped out to the street where his car was parked. He got in and put the key in the ignition, so he could start it right away if he had to. He sat there for about twenty minutes, trying to figure how badly he was hurt. He didn't feel as though any of his bones were broken, but all the organs in his body throbbed.

Eventually, he started the car. His hands trembled as they held the wheel, but he could drive. He got on the highway and headed for Santa Fe.

— * —

It was about eleven at night when he walked into the living room, where Miguel was sitting on the couch, watching a movie. Miguel took one look at him and said, "Oh, fuck. What happened?"

"You were right. The bikers are big on violence."

"Oh, man." Miguel stood up, put an arm around the Kid and helped him lie down on the couch. "How many were there?"

"Just one."

"Oh, man. You want something to drink? Water or something?"

"Can I have a beer?"

"Yeah, sure." Miguel went to the fridge, got two bottles of Samuel Adams and gave one to the Kid. "You need to go to the hospital?"

"No. I think I'm okay."

"I told you, bro. Give it up. There's other ways to make money. No need to get hurt. It ain't worth it."

— * —

Four days later, Crowley was coming out of Evangelo's, a bar just down the street from the Plaza in Santa Fe. The first thing he realized was that someone was sitting on his Harley. The second thing he realized was that it was the Kid.

"You know something? Some little bastards just can't be told," Crowley said.

"Nice bike," said the Kid.

"Get your brown ass off of it."

The Kid obeyed. Then he reached into his jacket and pulled out a Bulldog 44. He pointed it at Crowley.

Crowley cackled. "New toy, huh?"

"Yeah. Just got it."

"You know how to use it?"

"Not really. But it holds five rounds. I don't think I can miss you with all of them."

"That what you're gonna do, shoot me? Right here in the street, in front of people?"

"Yeah."

"Better go ahead, then."

The Kid gripped the gun in both hands to steady himself, and squeezed the trigger. The sound of the shot slapped his eardrums. He didn't see where the bullet hit Crowley. It wasn't like in the movies. Crowley didn't cry out or stagger backwards. He went straight down, as if a trap door had sprung open underneath him. He made no sound. He was immediately saturated in blood and red piss.

People passing by on the street, who at first hadn't noticed what was going on, now screamed and ran around. The Kid bent down, reached into Crowley's pocket and pulled out his wallet. It was slick with blood. The Kid holstered the gun, covered it with his jacket and walked away. He walked down to Water Street, where he'd left his car.

— * —

"You are fucking messing with me, bro," said Miguel.

The Kid shook his head.

"You fucking killed him?"

"Yeah, I think so. I didn't wait to find out." The Kid had found $314 in Crowley's wallet. He handed Miguel $100. He owed someone else $160 for the gun, but he wouldn't have to pay until he could afford it. "Look," he told Miguel. "You've been cool letting me stay here and eat your food and shit. I owe you this money. But if I'm gonna be wanted for murder and the bikers're gonna be looking for me, I don't blame you if you don't want me here no more. I'm gonna take off."

Miguel threw the money back at him. "Don't give me your shit. This is your house, okay? You can stay till you get somewhere. Just don't tell Mikey, huh?" Mikey was Miguel's roommate. "He's kind of uptight about killing people."

They watched the local news on TV. Crowley was dead, shot on the street by an unidentified Mexican male. The motive for the killing was not known, but there was speculation that it was drug-related.

"Good," the Kid said. "That means the bikers'll know about it and back off."

"They might not," Miguel said. "The bikers stick together. They got this code, you fight one, you got to fight them all."

"That's 'cause they don't expect to get killed. If any more of them want to get into it with me, that's up to them."

Miguel just looked at him and said nothing. He tried to imagine what had happened, what it had looked like. The Kid was sitting in an armchair, wearing blue jeans and a short-sleeved flannel shirt and running shoes. His hair was neatly combed. He was drinking coffee from a mug. Miguel looked at him and tried to see something that separated the Kid from everyone else, but he couldn't see it.

"What was it like?" he asked. "How did you feel?"

"I didn't care."

That was true, but it wasn't the whole truth. After it had happened, the Kid had sat in the Aztec Café and thought about it, what he had done, tried to take it all in. He'd thought he would be changed somehow, but he wasn't. It didn't seem like a big deal. He kept replaying it in his head, trying to feel some awe. But the awe never came. He'd never seen anyone die before, not even peacefully, and he'd always thought it would be dramatic, a life ending, maybe a spirit leaving the body. All that had happened was that Crowley was gone, dead, no change except that the body was broken and wouldn't function any more. It seemed like any other day. The café's hot cider tasted like it always did.

SIX

The cops pulled in some suspects, but none were guilty and the cops knew it. They never even talked to the Kid. Word had spread through the barrio that the Kid had done it, and would kill anyone else who went up against him, but nobody was sure it was true, and those who knew it was true weren't going to say anything to the cops. If anyone was going to snitch, it wouldn't have been to the cops—they would have made themselves some money by telling the bikers where he was. But nobody knew where he was, and the cops didn't know what to believe.

The Kid stayed at Miguel's. They never told Mikey what the Kid was into, but Mikey wasn't stupid. He got scared and decided to move out, so the Kid stopped being a guest, moved off Miguel's bedroom floor and into Mikey's room, and started sharing the rent.

He could afford it. He was making money. Some said it was from dealing, which he was definitely doing, and others said it was from killing people for money, which he may have been doing.

The bikers didn't like it, but they learned to accept it. Crowley had been the one who established control of the local drug trade, and with him dead there was no one among the bikers with the savvy to do it. The Kid's business wasn't large, and there was still enough of the market for the bikers. They knew it looked bad that a boy had faced them down by himself, but a couple of encounters with him helped the bikers decide they didn't want a feud. They talked a lot about killing him, but no one knew how to find him, and no one volunteered to try. There were even some bikers who believed that the Kid didn't exist, that he was a legend created in the barrio, a phantom who was blamed for every unsolved act of violence by a Mexican.

— * —

There are now some Latino gangs who claim the Kid, who say that he was down with them. The truth is that the Kid never claimed anyone but himself, and was never down with anyone except for the one or two people that he loved. When he was still in school, a couple of gangs did offer him membership, the chance to be jumped in—which means being beaten senseless as an initiation ceremony. The Kid said no, and the gangs left him alone because they had members who liked him. He belonged to no one, and now he seems to belong to everyone.

— * —

One evening Miguel said, "I think I'm gonna be your partner, bro."
"How come?"
"Going to work's easy, but coming home ain't, because of you."
"Why? What am I doing?"
"You sure as hell ain't selling advertising, that's for sure."
"What's wrong with selling advertising? I thought you liked it."
"It's not bad. But I got into it 'cause I ain't into getting killed or going to jail. Thanks to your fine efforts, it don't look like I'd have to worry about that no more, now that you've restored free enterprise to the Santa Fe narcotics trade."
"You always have to worry about it."
"Yeah, but . . . My problem ain't selling advertising. It's that I sell advertising all day, then I come home, and here you are. And what're you doing? You're laying around on your ass reading a damn book or whacking off to porno—if you ain't already in bed with some bitch. And that's all you've been doing all day long. That, my brother, is the problem. It makes me feel unfulfilled."
"So what're you gonna do about it?"
"Go in with you. You down with that?"
"Sure."
Miguel gave notice at the paper, telling his colleagues that he was going into business for himself, but neglecting to specify the nature of the business. They threw a party for him in a bar, and the Kid went along. Miguel introduced the Kid as his new business partner. When people asked what they were going to do, the Kid was cryptic, saying he liked to keep a lid on things. The sales guys looked suitably impressed.

The business built very quickly. Soon they had people working for them. They'd take business trips to Mexico. Sometimes their associates in Mexico would call and tell the Kid that they'd like him to visit a troublesome person in another state, and the Kid would always go. This was how he built favor. Miguel was an equal partner, but he knew he couldn't have done it by himself, or with another partner. It was people's fear of the Kid, and his usefulness to the narcos, that made it so easy. Miguel liked living with the Kid. They got along, and the Kid cooked dinner every night. Miguel had never eaten so well before. After dinner they'd go out to clubs and try to get laid. They were successful as often as not.

They became known to the cops and to the Drug Enforcement Administration. But the DEA was very good at identifying drug dealers and very poor at gathering enough evidence to arrest them. It was unusual for the Kid and Miguel to have the product they were selling in their house. And the cops had the wrong idea about what they were doing; they thought it was gang-related. A couple of times, they ambushed their suspects and searched them for tattoos. Miguel had some, so that proved that he was in a gang. The Kid didn't have any, which proved that he was in a gang too, but trying to hide the fact, or else he would have tattoos.

— * —

On one of the Kid's business trips south of the border, he stayed at a resort. It was an old resort and hardly exclusive, but that was something he liked about it. He would never have felt comfortable in a very formal surrounding, a place where he would have to think about etiquette all the time. This place wasn't like that. It was quite expensive, elegant but not grand, and being there made the Kid feel good.

The night after his business was taken care of, he was sitting by himself in the resort's jazz bar, listening to the house band. He saw a woman sitting alone at a table. She was white, blonde, in her twenties. She was looking at the Kid and smiling. He went over and asked if he could sit at her table. She kept smiling and said yes.

The woman was from Texas. She had just finished medical school, and was taking a vacation to reward herself. She was unhappy and wanted to talk about her life: loneliness, an abortion, a miserable relationship she was still involved with and couldn't seem to get herself to leave. The Kid listened as she talked. They ordered a bottle of red wine and drank it. The woman ate an avocado salad. The Kid had no counsel to offer her. Under the table, their legs were touching.

It got late. The band finished playing. She leaned close to the Kid and said, "I know I shouldn't, but I really want to kiss you right now."

The Kid kissed her on the mouth. Then they were kissing each other, their mouths open. He briefly felt her tongue before they moved apart.

"Let's finish these and go somewhere," the Kid said, pointing to their drinks.

"Okay . . . But I don't want to go to my room. Or your room. Let's just take a walk."

The resort had gardens, with lights and a fountain. They walked around, holding hands under a full moon. There was a dark, wooded area nearby. When the Kid walked towards it, the woman followed him.

When they were as far into the trees as they felt they needed to be, they stopped walking. The Kid took off his jacket, laid it on the ground, and they sat on it. They kissed, and kept kissing for a long time. She moaned into his mouth. He could feel the vibrations on her breath. He ran his hands down her shoulders to her waist, pulled her shirt out of her pants. He touched the skin at the small of her back, then slid a hand down into her pants. With his other hand, he reached for her belt and began to unfasten it.

She stopped him. "I can't," she said. "It's too much."

"Okay," he said. They went on kissing. After a while, her legs had parted and his hand had moved between them. He stroked her, harder as her moans got louder. She clung to him, rocking against him, eyes closed. Finally she gave an explosive gasp, then leaned her head on his chest.

"Did you come?" he asked her.

"No. I nearly did. But I can't relax."

"I want you to." He reached for her and began stroking her again, faster and more insistent.

"Oh shit . . ." She unfastened her belt and undid her pants. He put a hand inside her panties and felt her wetness squeeze around his fingers. She took his hand and moved it up a little, showing him where she felt it most. He stroked her and she came in seconds, squealing through clenched teeth.

They held each other and kissed for a while. Then he felt her get excited again.

"What do you want?" he whispered.

"I want to go," she said, her breathing so heavy that he could barely make out the words.

"What?"

"I want to go."

"Why?"

"I have to get back to my room. It's late. I'm just kind of . . . overwhelmed. I need to be by myself."

He kissed her. She rubbed against him, then pulled away. "I have to go. I'm going now."

The Kid didn't go with her. He sat on the ground and watched as she walked towards the gardens. At one point she looked back, smiled and waved. The Kid was sitting in the dark, and he didn't know if she could see him as he waved back.

He sat there for a while, then stood up, put on his jacket, and walked back to the gardens. He went to the fountain and sat on the edge. He wanted it always to be like this, the light exploding off the dark water and the brilliant moonlight all around. It wasn't just because of her, the lovely warm blonde realness of her, her smell still on him, her taste still on his fingers when he put them in his mouth. It was all of it—what they had just done, in a place where the language wasn't his. It was all so far away from his father and mother and their street where everyone's breath and clothes smelled of cigarettes, and everyone was either just out of the hospital or waiting to go in. The Kid was happy by the fountain because he didn't feel scared. He thought he had left his father's house and, wherever he went in the world, he would always be free of it.

— * —

The business lasted for about two years. There had been a delay in a consignment they were waiting for, and at around one o'clock in the morning they got a phone call from the guy who was carrying it. He asked if they wanted to meet him at a Denny's. The Kid was tired, and Miguel had a woman in bed with him, so the Kid told the guy to just come over to the house and drop it off.

He did. The Kid quickly drank a beer with him, then sent him on his way. He left the meth on the kitchen table and went back to bed. The woman Miguel was with didn't know what they were into, but the Kid figured he'd get up before them and move the stuff.

He didn't know the guy was a snitch.

At just after five in the morning, there was a banging on the front door. The Kid ignored it, but it didn't stop. Groggily, he got out of bed and, naked, went into the hall and stumbled towards the door. Before he reached it, it was smashed open, hit so hard that it bounced against the wall and slammed shut before being kicked open again. There were five cops, and they had a warrant. They also had their guns out.

They forced Miguel and his woman, Maria, to get out of bed. They herded everyone into the living room. Miguel was wearing shorts, and Maria was wearing his robe. The Kid was still naked. "Put something on," one of the cops told him.

"Yes, sir," said the Kid. He walked over to the stereo and looked at the rack of CDs. "Is Johnny Cash okay?"

The cop punched him in the face, sending him sprawling on the floor.

"Don't do that!" Maria yelled at the cop. "You didn't have to hit him."

"I felt that my life was in danger and used the minimum necessary force," the cop deadpanned.

The Kid stayed on the floor, thinking that if he got up the cop might knock him down again. He didn't feel afraid, just hopeless. He knew his life was over. He knew there was enough meth on the kitchen table to guarantee him and Miguel at least ten years each. He felt sad for Miguel, that he'd gotten him into this and ruined the good thing he had going with his job.

"Get up," another cop told him. The Kid got to his feet, warily, and the cop pulled his hands behind his back and cuffed him. Other cops did the same to Miguel and Maria.

"Okay," said the cop who had hit the Kid. "Do you want to do it nice and tell us where the drugs are?"

"We ain't got no drugs," the Kid said.

The cop shrugged. "Okay." They were led to the kitchen and made to sit at the table while the cops searched the house. The meth was right there on the table, under their noses, but they didn't notice it as they forced their prisoners to sit there and warned them not to move.

The cops trashed the place. They emptied drawers and closets and the contents of the fridge onto the floor, slit mattresses to look inside them. The Kid and Miguel sat and looked at each other. They looked at the meth, then back at each other. The Kid thought about telling the cops the stuff was right here, on the table, so they wouldn't do any more damage to the furniture. He knew it wouldn't matter much to him or Miguel what happened to the furniture—they weren't going to be needing it where they were going—but he didn't like seeing things being destroyed. But the thought was fleeting. Let them earn their paychecks.

Maria didn't do drugs, and so neither the Kid nor Miguel knew whether she realized what was on the table in front of her. She made to ask Miguel something, probably along the lines of What the fuck is going on? but he shook his head and whispered to her, telling her to just be cool and sit there and not say anything.

As they looked at each other, the Kid and Miguel felt as though they could read each other's minds. It was like a silent discussion. Both considered trying to somehow hide the drugs. Both considered the fact that they were in handcuffs, and that the only place the cops didn't seem to be looking was the kitchen table. And both decided not to do anything, to just pretend the drugs didn't exist.

The Kid felt a surge of hope rise inside him, and he tried to fight it down. He didn't want to hope. He knew he was going to prison, that the cops had only missed the drugs so far because they were busy searching everywhere else. He knew that, but the hope rose anyway.

The three of them sat at the table for more than an hour. They didn't speak. Then, at last, the cops came back into the kitchen. The Kid felt a lightness in his head and a jumping in his stomach.

The most senior cop leaned on the table, his face close to the Kid's, his hands almost touching the bags of meth. "All right," he said. "Where is it?"

"I don't know," the Kid said. The cop made to hit him, and the Kid shrank away. "Look, I ain't being smart. I don't know what you're looking for, I swear."

The cops took the Kid and Miguel into the living room. They left Maria handcuffed in the kitchen. They worked both of them over, not to try to get them to confess to anything, just because they wanted to. When they were done, they removed the handcuffs. They went to the kitchen and uncuffed Maria. Then they left.

Maria went into the living room. Miguel and the Kid both had puffy faces and bloody noses, but they were in each other's arms, laughing and crying at the same time, stomping their feet on the floor.

"We're going to fucking church, bro!" Miguel said through swollen lips. "I ain't kidding! In fact, you know what?—We're gonna pray now. I'm fucking serious, I swear to God. Right fucking now. On your knees." He looked at Maria. "You too, sweetie."

"Why?" she said.

"Because you just saw a fucking miracle! The Lord saved our sorry-assed fucking souls!"

"I'm a believer now," the Kid said.

Bemused, Maria joined them in kneeling on the floor, surrounded by the debris of the police search.

"Okay," Miguel said. "Lord, we thank thee for giving us each day our daily bread. We ask thee to forgive us our sins and help us be good people. We especially thank thee for making the cops too fucking dumb to notice four bags of meth when it's right in front of their faces. Amen."

"Amen," said the Kid.

"So you guys are drug dealers?" said Maria.

Miguel looked at the Kid. "Now that," he said, "is something we really need to have a talk about, bro. Know what I'm saying?"

"Yeah," said the Kid.

— * —

The Kid called the guy who'd snitched on them. "Hey," he said. "Guess where I'm calling from? I'll give you a clue. It ain't jail."

"Why would you be in jail?" the guy said, and the Kid heard it in his voice.

The Kid laughed. "You fucking idiot. You better pack your bags."

"Dude, I don't know what you're talking about."

"A bullet in the face."

"What?"

"That's what you're gonna get if you stay around."

"Why? From who?"

"From me, and you know why. Now, you better be gone before I find you."

Silence. Then the guy said, "I'm engaged. I'm gonna have a family. I can't go anywhere."

"You don't go anywhere, you ain't gonna get married and have a family. You're gonna be dead. I'll kill her too. I'll kill her first."

"What can I do? Just tell me."

"Nothing. You can leave or die."

He started to cry. "How long?"

"I'll be looking for you tomorrow."

"Okay. I'll be gone."

"Good idea. And don't come back." The Kid hung up.

— * —

That evening, the Kid and Miguel walked from their house to the Cowgirl Hall of Fame. There was live music that night, some shit-kicker cowpunk band, and there was a three-dollar cover charge. The guy on the door looked at their cut and beaten faces as they paid, but he said nothing. They went inside and got beers, then sat at a table outside.

"So, what do you think?" said Miguel.

"I don't know. What do you think?"

"I've had it, that's what I think."

The Kid nodded and didn't say anything.

"I mean, that was fucking close. That was as close as I want to get. If they'd found the shit, I don't know how long we were looking at—"

"I do. At least ten years."

"Jesus. That ain't funny. You know, after they'd gone, I just kept looking at Maria, and imagining not being able to see her, not being able to walk down the street or do anything for years . . . Man." Miguel shook his head.

"I think I'm with you. I think I'm gonna stop. What're you gonna do?"

"Selling advertising sudden looks pretty damn good," said Miguel. "You?"

"Don't know. I never thought about it before. There's enough money to get by on for a little while."

"Yeah." Miguel laughed. "It was good, huh? While it lasted. It was real fucking good."

The Kid smiled at him. "Yeah," he said. "It really was."

Miguel held out his hand. The Kid shook it.

"Let's go check out the band," Miguel said.

They went inside. It was busy. They ordered more beers, then stood watching the band. Miguel wasn't crazy about the music, but the Kid liked it. The beer started to give him a buzz. He thought that the occasion should seem momentous, but it didn't. He'd decided to quit what he'd been doing for two years, and it didn't seem to make any difference. He had a feeling of relief, that he wouldn't have to worry anymore, worry that the cops would bust him or that someone would kill him. He'd often wished he could be like Miguel, who never worried about anything and never made a big deal out of anything. He knew that Miguel would blithely go back to selling advertising or perhaps do something else and not even think about it. Nobody knew it, but the Kid was always afraid.

He thought about an afternoon a few weeks earlier. He'd been doing some business in Albuquerque, and was now driving back to Santa Fe. It was a warm day, and he drove with all the windows rolled down. He hung his left arm out of the window, and watched the concrete and desert go by. He felt good, but there was a sadness under the good feeling. He wished he wasn't afraid all the time. He wished he could just enjoy the day and not wonder how many more times he'd see it before a prison cell or a bullet took it all away.

Now he wouldn't have to be afraid. When the band had finished playing, the Kid and Miguel went back outside, but it was so crowded they couldn't find a table. So they stood, drank more beer, and talked. Some people they knew were there, and they waved to them and said hello. When the bar stopped serving, they decided to leave. Miguel went to take a piss, and the Kid waited for him.

The Kid noticed a woman sitting with two guys. They were all about his age. She looked like she was a mix of Mexican and Indian. Her straight hair was black, and reached almost to her waist. Her skin was light brown, and she had huge, slightly slanted eyes over high cheekbones. She was small and skinny, wearing blue denim shorts, black tights, a jacket, and a T-shirt.

She was looking at the Kid.

"What happened to your face?" she said.

"Got beat up," he said, unable to think of a plausible lie.

"Who by?"

"Some guys."

She pointed to the space on the bench beside her. "Sit down."

He did. She introduced him to the two guys. "This is Martin, but I call him Martian. And this is Bobby."

The Kid shook hands with them both, and told them his name.

"My name's Vanjii," the woman said. The two guys went on talking with each other. She kept looking at the Kid, and said, "Why'd you get beat up?"

"No reason. They were just messing with us."

"Did they beat up that guy you're here with too?"

"Yeah."

"Where's he?"

"At the restroom."

"Hey, can I ask you a question?"

"Yeah."

"Are you and him like . . . gay?"

The Kid laughed at the thought. "No, we're both straight. What made you think that?"

"I saw you both coming out of Trash Disco once. A lot of gay guys go there."

"Well, not us. He's my roommate."

She smiled at him. "I'm glad you're straight." She lowered her voice. "Neither of these guys is my boyfriend, they're just friends. Bobby wants to be, but it's never gonna happen."

Miguel appeared. "Hey, bro. We leaving or staying?" he asked the Kid.

Before the Kid could answer, Vanjii said, "Martian's giving me a ride home. Hey, you doing anything tomorrow?"

"Not really," the Kid said.

"Well, I'll be working at Woolworth's in the Plaza. Come and see me in the afternoon, okay?"

"Okay."

Before he stood up, she hugged him quickly.

The Kid and Miguel walked out into the street. "How in the hell did you get talking to her?" Miguel asked.

"I didn't. She got talking to me."

"Man. Today has been the best of times and worst of times for sure."

"Where'd you get that?"

"It's from the book I'm working on," Miguel said.

The Kid looked at him. "You're writing a book?"

"Hell, no. I'm trying to read one."

They both laughed, half-realizing how drunk they were. The Kid told Miguel what Vanjii had said to him, and Miguel had hysterics. "If it was anybody but you, I'd say they had to be messing with me. Come and see me at Woolworth's . . . God damn."

SEVEN

The Kid slept until around eleven, then got up and ate fried chicken livers and eggs for breakfast. Miguel was still asleep. The Kid drank some coffee, then went outside and got in his car. He drove to Acequia Madre Street, to the house where the snitch lived. He parked, got out of the car and knocked on the door.

A young woman opened it. "Is Rob home?" the Kid asked her.

She looked at him venomously. "He left."

"When'll he be back?"

"He won't be back. He left for good."

"Where'd he go?"

"I don't know. He didn't say where he was going."

The Kid knew she was lying, but that didn't matter. "Thanks," he said. The woman closed the door. The Kid wondered if she was the woman the snitch had planned to marry, and if she would join him wherever he was moving to.

— * —

The Kid drove to the Plaza, but in the early afternoon it was impossible to find a parking space anywhere near it. He drove around for a while, then headed for the Aztec Café. He drank a hot cider and read the *New Mexican*. It wasn't a very long walk from Aztec Street to the Plaza, so when he left the Aztec he decided to leave his car there and walk.

The Woolworth's was made from adobe, but the Kid didn't know whether it was real. A lot of the buildings are just made that way for the benefit of tourists and white incomers. Only rich white people lived in the center of town now; gentrification had driven the Mexicans out into the barrios. The Kid went into the Woolworth's and looked at the checkout people, but none of them was Vanjii. He walked around the store looking for her among the aisles, but he didn't find her.

Then he heard her yell, "Hey!"

There was a snack bar to one side of the store. She was standing behind the counter, waving to him. She wore a uniform, and her hair was in a long ponytail.

The Kid walked over to the counter. "Hey," he said.

She came around from behind the counter and hugged him like they were old friends. "I didn't think you'd show up," she said.

"Why not?"

She laughed. "I don't know. I just didn't. Hey, you want something to eat?" She lowered her voice. "My boss ain't around, so you can have it for free."

"Yeah, thanks." The Kid didn't relish the prospect of eating anything from a Woolworth's menu, but he didn't want to be impolite. He scanned the menu. "I guess I'll have a hot dog and some fries and a Dr Pepper."

"You got it. Sit down and I'll bring it to you."

He sat in a booth. Vanjii brought him his food about two minutes later. She put the tray on the table in front of him, then sat down facing him.

"Tell me something," he said. "Did you go to Capitol High School?"

"Yeah," she said. "Did you?"

"Yeah."

"That's weird. I don't remember you."

Just as well, the Kid thought. "I kind of remember you," he said. "But I wasn't sure."

"I had short hair back then."

"You sure don't now."

"I know. I haven't cut it in six years."

"It's really cool, though. I like it."

"Cool," she said.

"What time do you get off work?"

"At four."

"You want to go do something?"

"Yeah. What do you wanna do?"

"I don't care. Anything you want. What kind of music do you like?"

The Kid shrugged. "Everything. How about you?"

"The same. You wanna go up to the Paramount tonight?"

"Sure. What's going on there?"

"I don't know. There'll be something. Or I think there's a punk show at Doctor Know."

"Whatever you want," he said.

Someone called to her. There were other customers she had to serve. "I have to get back to it," she told the Kid. "You gonna come back later, or hang out here until I'm done?"

The Kid looked at his watch. It was just past two. "I'll hang out here, if that's okay with you."

"Cool. You don't have to work today?"

"No. I just quit my job."

He went and bought a magazine, then came back to the booth, sat down, and read it. Whenever things got slow, Vanjii would come over and talk to him.

"What was the job you quit?" she said.

"I had my own business, me and my friend Miguel you saw with me last night. We were selling advertising, but it didn't work out."

"Yeah? So what're you gonna do now?"

"I don't know yet. I'm thinking about it."

"Hey, do people call you the Kid? Is that your nickname?"

"Yeah, I guess. Who told you?"

"My friend Bobby. Remember, he was with me last night? He told me."

"What else did he tell you?"

"Just stuff. That you're bad news. But Martian says he's just jealous 'cause he knew I wanted to hang out with you."

"Did what he said bother you?"

"Nah." She smiled at him.

When she finished her shift, she asked him, "Do you have a car?"

"Yeah."

"Well, can you do me a favor? My car's at my apartment. I got drunk and crashed at Martian's last night, and he drove me here today. I was gonna call him or Bobby and get them to pick me up and give me a ride, but I'd rather just hang out with you . . ."

"Yeah, I'll drive you. But my car's down on Aztec Street. You mind walking down there?"

"No, I like walking. I ain't been driving much, since I got my license suspended."

"What for?"

"DUI. I got pulled over so drunk I was driving the wrong way on a one-way street."

The Kid laughed. "I did that once when I was sober."

Vanjii took off her uniform smock. Under it she wore a T-shirt. She was also wearing black jeans and Doc Marten boots. She put on a leather jacket, and she and the Kid went outside.

"So how long've you worked at Woolworth's?" he said as they walked.

"About six months. I ain't gonna do it much longer. It sucks. I was going to the community college but I ran out of money, so I quit and started working full-time. I thought I could save enough money to go back to school, but I don't make enough."

"What do you want to do after you go to school?"

"Don't know," she said.

She told him she was born in Santa Fe, but when her parents split up her mother had taken the kids to Phoenix for a few years. They'd come back to Santa Fe when Vanjii was thirteen, and she had been there ever since. She was always thinking about moving to Phoenix, or maybe just to Albuquerque, anywhere that wasn't Santa Fe, but she never seemed to make the move.

As she walked, Vanjii talked fast, with hardly a pause for breath. Every now and then she'd turn her head away and spit, but she didn't let that break the flow of her sentences. Unlike many women, she wasn't as tall as the Kid, and he liked that. On every other street they walked down, someone would wave to her and she would yell, "Hey!" and wave back.

They reached Aztec Street and got in the Kid's car. He followed Vanjii's directions. She had a room in a shared house in the barrio, not very far from his parents' place. "I'm beat," she said as he parked the car in the driveway. "I wanna take a nap. How about you?"

"Yeah, I'm tired," he said. He wasn't tired at all, but he liked the idea of lying down with her, if that was what she had in mind.

It was. Her room was little more than a closet. Her clothes were strewn everywhere. There was a quilt on the bed, but no sheet. They took off their jackets and shoes and lay on the bare mattress and covered themselves with the blanket. "We can sleep for a while, then eat something, then go out," Vanjii said. "Okay?"

"Uh-huh."

They lay close together. The Kid put an arm around Vanjii. She didn't seem to mind. He kissed her face, then her mouth. She kissed him back lightly, but didn't open her mouth, and pulled away when he tried to kiss her harder. "Go to sleep," she said.

She turned away from him, lying on her side. He kept on holding her, snuggling from behind, liking the feel of her ass against his groin. She smelled of soap or shampoo or lotion, he didn't know which and didn't care.

Vanjii fell asleep quickly. The Kid lay there for more than an hour, awake, wanting her, but glad of the little he had. One of his hands was on her stomach. He could feel the heat of her skin through the fabric of her shirt, feel her breathing. He found himself imagining how easily she could be turned into nothing, how a bullet or a blade could open her body and turn it into cold meat, take away everything she was. Holding her, he couldn't believe that was true, but he knew it was.

Then he fell asleep too.

When he woke, the room was dark. She was awake too. It was the sound of her breathing that woke him. She was lying on her back, taking big, painful, wheezing breaths.

"What's wrong?" he said.

She didn't answer. He asked again, and she said, "I can't breathe. It hurts."

"Why?"

". . . I don't know."

"Do you need to go to the hospital?"

"I don't know."

But the Kid knew. Vanjii was so weak she could hardly sit up. "I'm gonna call an ambulance," the Kid said.

"Don't. They charge you five hundred dollars. My tia died last month, and they sent my cousin the bill."

"Okay. Then I'm gonna drive you."

"I ain't got insurance."

"You're going anyway. Look at you."

They put on their jackets and shoes. The Kid looked around the house, hoping one or more of her roommates might be home and be able to help. But the house was dark and empty. The Kid half-led, half-carried Vanjii to his car. She lay down on the back seat and curled up.

It was cold, and the car's engine died the first couple of times the Kid started it. When it caught and stayed alive, he sat and let it warm up for a minute. He could hear Vanjii shivering.

He had never been sick, so he didn't know any hospitals. He asked Vanjii, and she told him to take her to St. Vincent's. He'd heard of it. People called it St. Victim's. As he drove, he asked Vanjii how she was doing. She didn't answer, just kept taking these shallow, wheezing breaths.

He parked the car and helped her to the emergency room. She told the receptionist what was wrong. The receptionist asked if she'd been treated there before, and Vanjii said yes. The receptionist punched her name into the computer. "Is your insurance still with Cigna?" she said.

That insurance had been provided by one of Vanjii's past employers, and had long since lapsed, but Vanjii didn't feel the need to say so. "Yeah."

The receptionist handed her some forms and told her to fill them out.

In her state, it took Vanjii more than ten minutes to complete the forms. When she handed them back to the receptionist, she was told to sit down and wait to be called. There were rows of chairs in the reception area. The Kid sat down. Vanjii curled up on the seats beside him and rested her head in his lap. She closed her eyes. He stroked her hair.

Vanjii's breathing got more painful. The Kid watched her, and noticed that, between each spasmodic inhalation and explosive exhalation, there seemed to be a moment when she wasn't hurting. The Kid remembered something he'd read somewhere about breathing.

"Hey," he murmured to her. "I thought of something. If it's hurting you to breathe, try holding it."

"What do you mean?"

"I think you try to wait a little bit before you breathe out . . . I think you breathe in, then hold it a little, then breathe out."

She tried it and found that it helped. It hurt to breathe in, and hurt almost as much to breathe out again. But the time in between didn't hurt at all. Doing that made her breath slow down a little, so that all the pain lessened. She closed her eyes, her cheek pressed against the Kid's thigh. She could smell laundry soap from his jeans. The hand he stroked her hair with didn't smell of anything, it was just warm.

A nurse called her. "Evangelina?"

She sat up. "Yeah."

"Follow me."

Vanjii looked at the Kid. "Can my friend come with?"

"Not right now. Maybe later."

"I'll wait here," the Kid told Vanjii.

She was gone for more than an hour. He wished he had something to read. There was a TV set in the waiting area, but it wasn't showing any programs. What it showed was videos of different diseases, to scare people into buying insurance. There were so many things that could kill you, the Kid wondered that anyone was still alive. He found himself developing psychosomatic symptoms of every ailment he saw on the screen.

Three teenage kids, a boy and two girls, were sitting across from him. The Kid listened to their conversation, and realized that they had a relative who was very ill. They cried and smiled at each other. They obviously hadn't met before. "You know I'm your cousin, right?" one girl said to the other. The Kid felt envious of them. He wanted to sit with them, be part of it.

A man in his forties appeared, and said something to them. The Kid gleaned that he was the husband of the sick woman, but couldn't tell whether the news was good or bad. They all left together.

A nurse told the Kid he could see Vanjii now. He found her sitting on the edge of a gurney, with a thermometer sticking out of her mouth. She looked comical, and he knew that she must be feeling better; he could tell that she had lost her fear and was getting her attitude back.

"How're you doing?" he said.

"I'm okay."

"Did they tell you what's wrong with you?"

"Yeah. I've got bronchitis and pleurisy."

"Shit. What can they do about it?"

"They gave me some drugs. And they gave me a prescription."

"You don't have to stay in the hospital?"

"No. Anyway, I want to get out of here before they realize my insurance ain't for real."

They left the hospital, the Kid with an arm around Vanjii's shoulders. "What was it made you get sick?"

"Don't know," she said. "I've always been kind of weak in the lungs." She grinned at him. "But it ain't contagious."

"I wasn't worried about that." But he had been.

It was around ten o'clock. He drove to a supermarket that had a pharmacy, and she filled the prescription. The Kid paid for it, and she thanked him and didn't argue. In the parking lot, they sat in his car and he looked at her and said, "What do you want to do now?"

"I need to sleep. I have to work tomorrow."

"The shape you're in, you should take the day off. Call in sick."

"I can't afford to lose a day's pay."

"Well, I can take you home . . . or do you want to stay at my house tonight?"

He'd felt nervous about asking, but she wasn't fazed. "Yeah, that'd be cool."

— * —

Miguel wasn't home. The Kid and Vanjii sat in the kitchen and drank green tea.

"You know something?" Vanjii said. "You are fucking cool."

The Kid smiled. "How come?"

"You only just met me, and you take me to the hospital and sit there forever waiting for me . . . That's so cool."

"Maybe I just like hospitals," the Kid said, and they both laughed. The Kid moved his chair closer to hers and kissed her.

"Can I ask you something?" she said.

"Yeah."

"I know you like me . . . but do you *like me* like me? Like, I know you think I'm cute and stuff, but would you want to hang out with me a lot?"

"Yeah."

"For real?"

"Yeah."

"'Cause I really like you," she said. "And you don't have to say stuff just to get in bed with me, because I want to do that anyway. But I just want to know if you like me."

"Yeah."

They went to the Kid's bedroom. He turned on a lamp, and Vanjii looked around. The walls were white, and almost bare. There was a mirror, two photos of lowriders, and a painting of the Virgin of Guadalupe, done by a friend in prison. There were shelves of books, a stereo, piles of CDs, and a double bed.

The Kid was standing behind her. He put his arms around her waist, and she leaned back against him. They stayed like that for a moment, then she turned around and kissed him quickly. "Can we go to sleep?" she said. "I'm so tired."

The Kid went to the bathroom. When he came back, Vanjii was getting in bed. He saw that she was wearing her T-shirt and panties. He didn't know if that meant he shouldn't be naked, so he stripped to his boxer shorts and got in the bed. "Should I turn the light off?" he said.

"Yeah."

"Do you need me to set the alarm?"

"Well . . . I gotta work at noon."

He turned off the lamp. "I'll wake up way before then."

They snuggled together, kissed a little. The Kid began kissing Vanjii's neck, pressing himself against her. Her breathing got heavy, then she laughed and hunched her shoulders to stop him. "Okay, knock it off. You're getting me all hot."

"Good. I'm sure trying."

"Yeah, but I still don't feel so good. I need to sleep."

"Okay."

"I know that sounds lame."

"No, it doesn't."

She kissed him. "Plenty of time, huh?"

"Yeah."

She fell asleep, with one of the Kid's arms around her. He stayed awake for a while, listened to her breathing as she slept, listened to his own, and at some point he slept too.

— * —

He woke just before eight in the morning. Vanjii was still asleep and didn't look like waking up anytime soon. The Kid tried to go back to sleep, but couldn't, even though he still felt tired. He lay on his side and watched Vanjii sleep. Eventually, he eased himself out of bed and went to the kitchen. He was making coffee when Miguel came in.

"Hey," said the Kid. "Did you stay at Maria's?"

"I did indeed," Miguel said. He looked at the Kid's underwear. "You having problems getting your ass fully dressed this morning?"

"I got company . . ."

"I can guess who."

"Yeah. But I slept like this."

"You didn't get naked? You're a disappointment, bro. If you ain't got a dirty story for me, pour me some coffee instead."

The Kid obliged, and told him what had happened the day before. "Damn," said Miguel. "So she's in your bed right now?"

"Yeah. Keep your voice down. She might get up and hear you."

They sat together at the table and drank the coffee. "So, you figured out what you're gonna do next?" Miguel said.

"I ain't had time."

"I know who you wanna do next."

"You got that right."

"Think you're gonna?"

"Yeah. She said so. I just don't know when. Have you decided what you're gonna do?"

"Today, my brother, I'm going over to the *New Mexican* to ask my old boss if he got a job for me."

"Think he will?"

"Yeah, he'll make one for me. He's a good guy. And, hell, I'm good at selling shit."

When the Kid had finished his coffee, he went to the bathroom and brushed his teeth. Then he went to his bedroom.

Vanjii was still asleep. The Kid took off his shorts. She stirred a little as he got in the bed. She was lying on her side. He turned her on her back and she didn't resist. He tried to kiss her mouth, but she said, "My breath!" and turned her head away. He kissed her face and neck, and she put her arms around him. He felt her small tits through her T-shirt, then pulled the shirt up and licked the brown nipples. He sucked on one of them, biting it a little, and she liked it. He moved down, kissing her stomach, licking her navel. He pulled down the top of her panties and nuzzled her pubes. She lifted her hips as he pulled the panties down and off. She smiled as he pushed her legs apart and put his face between them.

It took her a long time to come, but the Kid didn't mind. He liked doing it to her, even though it took so long that his tongue began to ache. He stayed there for a while after she'd come, softly kissing the lips of her cunt. Then he turned her over and kissed her ass, slipping his tongue between the cheeks. She moaned and pushed back against him. "You like me fucking your face?" she said.

The Kid murmured something and probed deeper with his tongue. He reached under and stuck a finger in her cunt, fingering her while he licked her ass, and she came again, harder this time. He would have gone on licking, but she reached for him and pulled him up to lie beside her.

"That was cool," she said, and the Kid laughed.

"What's funny?" she said.

"You."

"How come?"

"I don't know. You just are."

They lay cuddled together, on their sides, her back to him. She could feel how hard he was. "You got a condom?" she asked, pressing her ass into him.

"No. I think my roommate might. I'll ask him." But, a second or two later, he moved his body a little bit lower, and his cock slid into her cunt.

"Don't," she said, but as she said it she reached back, grabbed his ass and pulled him deeper into her.

"Want me to stop?" he said.

"You should stop."

"Do you want me to?"

". . . No."

He held her by the hips and fucked her hard. "Don't come in me," she moaned.

"I won't."

He pulled out of her and came all over her ass and lower back. She continued to moan, more quietly now, as he rubbed the thick come into her skin and into her asscrack. Then he put his arms around her and held her close, kissing her ear and cheek.

"Did you like that?" she said.

"Yeah. Did you?"

"Yeah."

"Sorry I didn't make you come."

"You made me come twice."

"I mean just now."

"That's cool. I liked it anyway."

— * —

It was around ten o'clock when they got out of bed. Vanjii asked if she could take a shower, and the Kid told her to go ahead. He asked if she was hungry, and she said she was. The Kid said he'd make some risotto. She went into the bathroom. The Kid went to the kitchen and put some rice in a rice cooker. Then he went to the bathroom and knocked on the door. "Hey, can I come in?"

"Yeah," she called to him.

He opened the door. She was naked, sitting on the toilet, taking a piss. She grinned at the Kid. He went over to her, knelt in front of her and kissed her. Everything about her turned him on. He didn't have any toilet fetish that he knew of, but even the sight of her sitting there pissing excited him, and so did watching her wipe herself with a piece of toilet paper, flush, stand up, get in the bathtub, turn the shower on . . .

She closed the shower curtain. He opened it, got in there with her, closing the curtain behind him. He looked at the whiteness of the shampoo in the darkness of her hair. He put his arms around her. "No getting us all hot, okay?" she said. "I need to get to work." But when they washed each other and she was soaping his hard cock with her hand, it was too much for her, and she insisted that he fuck her right there in the shower. Then they rinsed themselves off in a hurry, wrapped themselves in towels, went back to the bedroom and put their clothes on.

In the kitchen, she watched him cook. He chopped an onion and a few slices of bacon, then cooked them together in a big skillet. Then he added the rice, stirring it so the bacon fat would get mixed in. He kept on stirring it as he added hot chicken stock, a cup at a time. "This is the important part," he told her. "You don't want to put a lot of stock in all at once, just enough to keep the rice from getting burned. You let it get absorbed into the rice, then you put in a little more."

"Cool. Who showed you how to do that?"

"Nobody. I read it in a book. Do you like to cook?"

"I guess. But I always use the same recipe."

"What recipe?"

"You open the can, pour it in the pot and put it on the stove."

The Kid laughed. "I can't eat stuff like that." He poured some more stock into the skillet and kept stirring. "You can't get stuff like this out of a can. Wait and see."

When she tasted it, she didn't argue. "This is awesome," she said.

"Yeah, thanks. My roommate Miguel says he can't eat his mom's cooking no more, since he started living with me."

"You always cook for him?"

"Yeah, usually. I like cooking for people. And he don't know how to cook."

"He lucked out getting you as a roommate."

"That's what he says. He's scared I'll get married or something and then he'll starve." The Kid laughed. "I keep telling him, learn to cook. It ain't hard."

"Will you show me?"

He looked at her. "Yeah."

EIGHT

Jesus Griego couldn't believe he was going to die. He'd been waiting for more than twenty years. Every time they were about to kill him, the lawyer did something, there was another delay, and it didn't happen. But now the lawyer was telling him that this time was different, that there would be no delay, that they were going to kill him. The lawyer was saying he was sorry, the appeals had been exhausted, and Jesus was trying to figure what he could say in return.

When Jesus was twenty, he was working in Phoenix, cleaning swimming pools for the white people. He drank, smoked pot, did speed, sniffed paint if he couldn't get anything else. He'd been getting high since he was ten. One Saturday afternoon he was driving his truck with a couple of friends a few miles outside of town. They picked up a hitchhiker, a guy in his forties. They drove into the desert, parked the truck and they all got out. Jesus and his friends told the guy to give them his money and ID. He did. The guy told them he was afraid of them, said he wouldn't call the cops, he just wanted to see his son grow up. They shoved him to the ground and kicked him until there was shit in his pants and brain fluid was leaking out of his nostrils. Jesus got an idea. He told his friends, "Check this out." He got in the truck and rolled it until one of the wheels was on the guy's head. Then he revved it, spinning the wheels. His friends laughed and cursed as they jumped back to avoid splashes of the dirty red soup the guy's head was turning into.

The prosecutor gave Jesus a choice. He could forgo his right to a trial, plead guilty, and he could be paroled within fifteen years. Or he could plead not guilty and take it to trial, in which case they'd press for the death penalty.

The public defender told him to accept the deal, told him that there was no chance of an acquittal, and that what he'd done easily met the criteria for the death penalty, that the murder be "especially heinous, cruel or depraved." But other people told Jesus that the public defender's job is always to talk the client into pleading guilty to avoid inconveniencing the courts. So he told him he wanted a trial. He got one, and the judge sentenced him to death.

Now the lawyer was telling him that it was going to happen. He couldn't feel afraid because he couldn't believe it. He was forty-two. The longer he lived, the less plausible it seemed that they could kill him for something he'd done when he was a kid. Other people on Arizona's death row in Florence prison, people he knew and was friends with, had been executed, so he knew it could happen, knew it was true. He knew it, but he didn't believe it.

"I'm very sorry, Jesus," his lawyer told him.

"It's okay. Thanks," Jesus said. He liked the lawyer, who worked at the Federal Public Defender's Office in Phoenix. Jesus liked to read, but in recent times death row inmates weren't allowed to have books. The lawyer had helped him out there by giving him books as, he claimed, a part of a legal brief, telling the authorities that he wanted his client to read contemporary literature in order to find passages that he would quote when he had to present his case at the clemency hearing. They knew it was bullshit, but there wasn't much they could do about it.

Now the lawyer was asking him what he wanted for his last meal, what he wanted done with his body, and who he wanted to invite to watch him die.

Jesus thought about it. He wasn't close to anyone in his family except for his niece Vanjii, who was his sister's daughter. He couldn't even say he was all that close to Vanjii either, but she still wrote to him regularly, and visited him sometimes. She was the only one who did. He wrote to her and invited her to come but told her he would understand if she didn't want to. She wrote back right away, telling him she would come if she could, but that her car would never get her from New Mexico to Arizona, that she didn't have enough money to rent a car, and that her license was suspended. He told her not to worry, that he would put her on his witness list so that she could attend if she was able to. He was allowed five other witnesses, but he couldn't think of anyone to invite. His lawyer and an investigator both offered to attend, and he thanked them and agreed.

A week before the day, a letter came from Vanjii. She said she had a new boyfriend, and he had offered to drive her to Arizona.

— * —

Silent night? Not ever, not around here, thought the Kid. It was midnight and he was in his bed, Vanjii asleep beside him. As usual, there had been the intermittent barking of dogs outside. Now there was a quarrel between a woman and a man. The man's voice was so low the Kid couldn't make out what he was saying, but he didn't have the same problem with the woman. "You piece of fucking shit . . . Yeah, you are, that's exactly what you are . . . You fucking take me for every dime I got, and you don't fucking care . . . You're gonna just do what you want . . . Yeah, well, fuck you, fuck you, fuck you . . . I don't even want you in my house . . . That's it, motherfucker, walk away, just walk away . . ." The Kid pressed his face into Vanjii's hair, grateful. He marveled at her ability to sleep through anything. He hoped to get some sleep himself before the morning, when they would get on the road to Arizona. He had never been there before, but he'd been told that the drive would take at least eight hours. On the floor of his bedroom, Vanjii's bag was packed and waiting.

— * —

They had given Jesus a mild sedative before they'd strapped him to the gurney. When they tried to put the catheters in his arm, they couldn't find a vein. So they dissected his arm. This procedure, which is called "cutting down," took about a half-hour. When it was done, the arm wasn't recognizable as an arm, but there were veins, and catheters stuck in them. They bound what remained so he wouldn't bleed to death. Then they wheeled the gurney, with Jesus strapped to it, into the execution room and left him there for twenty minutes.

He raised his head and looked around. To his right there was a big window, but it was covered with a curtain. He wondered whether the witnesses were already there, whether Vanjii was standing on the other side of the glass. He couldn't hear anything, but he knew the glass was soundproof.

He started to cry. Rather, he thought he was crying, but he wasn't sure. There were whimpering sounds coming out of his mouth, and he could feel snot coming out of his nose, and he knew he was going to piss in the diaper he was wearing. But his eyes didn't feel wet at all. All of last night he had imagined this, what it would be like, how it would feel, getting ready for it. But now it wasn't like anything he had imagined, and he wanted his mother to come and protect him. He tried to think about the man he had killed, tried to wonder whether the man had felt like this, but it was so long ago that he only vaguely remembered it.

They came back to the room and told him there had been no last-minute stay of execution. His nose and mouth were covered in snot. He asked one of them to wipe it away with a tissue. The guy took his glasses off, wiped his face, then replaced the glasses and asked if he wanted to keep them on. Jesus said yes. Then they all left, all except for the warden. Someone on the other side of the glass rolled back the curtain.

Jesus almost recoiled when he saw Vanjii. He couldn't believe how close she was, standing there looking at him, with her beautiful long hair and young face and pretty blue dress. She looked at him, showing nothing, and then she smiled. He smiled back. His lawyer, Chuck, was standing beside her. Chuck winked at him. There were other people there, but Jesus didn't know who they were.

On the car stereo, Robert Earl Keen sang, "Things ain't never what they seem/When you find you been livin' in your own dream." The car was parked on a dirt lot near the prison, but the Kid had the engine idling so that the air conditioning would run. But the air conditioning was weak, and the Kid had never felt heat like this, not even at the height of summer in Santa Fe. Everything was so bright, and the air seemed to be on fire. He had driven Vanjii up to the checkpoint, but they wouldn't let him go any further. They'd told him to wait for her down the road. He'd hoped to find a café nearby with air conditioning, but there wasn't one. He'd have to drive further into town for that, and he didn't want to not be there when Vanjii came out of the prison. So he sat where he was, listening to the stereo, watching the twenty or so people who were having a vigil to protest the death penalty. The execution was scheduled for three o'clock. It was now about a minute past.

— * —

As Vanjii stood facing the curtain, waiting for it to be opened, she thought it would be like watching a movie, that her uncle would be far away. When the guy pulled back the curtain, it wasn't like that at all. Her uncle was so close that she could almost have reached out and touched him if it hadn't been for the glass. He was covered by a sheet almost to his neck, so she couldn't see what had happened to his arm, and there was no sign of any tubes leading to him. He looked like he was lying in bed waiting for someone to bring him coffee and a newspaper. He was too big, too real, for it to be true.

A man came into the execution room. He stood at the foot of the gurney and looked at her uncle. A speaker was turned on, and she heard the man ask, "Inmate Griego, is there anything you'd like to say before the sentence is carried out?"

Her uncle looked at her, but she didn't know what kind of look it was. Then he looked at the man. "No," he said.

The speaker was turned off. The man left. Her uncle looked at her and smiled, then closed his eyes and turned his head away.

Vanjii watched him suffocate. His face seemed to swell and pull away from his head. It was as though a series of explosions were taking place under his skin. His lips flapped like clothes on a line being blown by the wind. She looked at Chuck. He put his arm around her. The blank expression on his face was melting, and she knew without asking that he had never lost a client before.

After about a minute, her uncle was just lying there, his face still. Vanjii was Catholic, and had expected to see some indication that he was leaving, going somewhere else, departing the ruined body. But there was nothing.

Everyone stood and looked at the body for a while. Then there was an announcement that the execution had been completed at 3:05. The curtain was closed.

Vanjii looked around her. In the front row, along with her uncle's witnesses, there were four relatives of the man he'd killed. One was a very old woman with an oxygen tube attached to her nose. She was crying. The others were men in their forties, and they just looked dumbfounded. The other rows were made up of reporters and some local political figures. Vanjii didn't know who they were. One of the reporters laughed and slapped the county attorney on the back, saying, "They finally got it done. That did my old heart good." The reporter's name was Jeremy Ruvin. At the time, Vanjii didn't know his name and had no reason to think she would ever see him again.

"I know Jesus was glad you came," Chuck said to her.

"Yeah."

"One of my colleagues was going to come too . . . I don't know why he didn't."

Vanjii didn't say anything.

"I did everything I could. I liked him."

"He told me you were good to him," she said.

— * —

The Kid saw Vanjii come walking down the road with a guy in a suit, who he figured must be her uncle's lawyer. When they got closer to where he was, they stopped and talked for a few minutes. Then they shook hands, and Vanjii walked to the Kid's car, opened the door on the passenger side, got in.

"Did they do it?" asked the Kid.

"Yeah."

"You okay?"

"Yeah." She leaned over and put her head on his shoulder. He put an arm around her.

"What do you want to do now?" He asked her. "Where do you want to go?"

"I don't care. But I don't want to stay here."

"Here? You mean Arizona, or just Florence?"

"Just Florence."

"How about we go to Phoenix, then? Since you lived there, and it's on the way home . . ."

"Yeah. That'd be cool."

The drive to Phoenix took a little more than an hour. As he drove, the Kid said, "I don't know what it was like for you, so I ain't gonna try to make you talk about it. If you don't want to, that's okay. But if you do want to, you can . . ."

"I know," she said. "It's not that I don't want to talk about it. I just don't know what to say about it. I don't even think anything about it. I don't know what to think."

"But you're okay?"

"Yeah."

— * —

She told him Phoenix wasn't the same as it had been when she lived there. It wasn't like anyplace he had ever seen in real life. It reminded him of science-fiction movies he'd seen, like maybe *Blade Runner*. The streets were jammed with cars, but there were no people on the sidewalks, nobody walking anywhere. Most of the residential streets didn't even have sidewalks. There were no individual stores or cafés or bars on the streets, only strip malls where such businesses were housed. It seemed as though every main street was lined with car dealerships. The streets were broad, the buildings were stucco, the sun was merciless, and the freeways cast shadows everywhere.

It had been a small town, and then a small city. But now it was the fifth-largest city in the country. Development was running riot and so was the homicide rate. Thousands of people were moving there every year, but few of them planned to stay. They just wanted to make some money while there was money to be made, before the water ran out and the boom gave way to a slump. Most of the money coming in never touched most of the people who lived there; Arizona is a "right to work" state, which means no right to job security, benefits, or a living wage. The media conducted polls that showed that half of the city's residents would leave if they could.

The Kid drove in on I-10, Vanjii sitting quietly beside him. "Where should we go?" he asked her as he took the Seventh Street exit.

"I don't know . . . Want to see where I used to live?"

"Yeah."

He followed her directions, and ended up outside an apartment complex at Fifteenth Avenue and Grand. The barrio was just south of the freeway, but the neighborhood on the north side was a million miles away. The houses on the north were big, expensive, and well maintained, and the residents, though they had brown skin, were white on the inside—they had money, and many of them didn't speak Spanish. To the south, the houses were small and faded, and there were liquor stores, pawnshops and single-occupancy motels.

The Kid parked the car on the street, and followed Vanjii into the complex. They stopped outside a ground-floor apartment. "This is it," she said. "Number five."

"How many rooms are there?"

"Two bedrooms. My mom had one, and me and my sister had the other one."

"Does it feel weird, being here now?"

"Nah. I was too little to really remember it now. C'mon." She started walking back to the car.

The Kid didn't know what to say to her. He had been seeing her for a month, and he had never known her to be quiet. He didn't know what would be the right thing to say to her about her uncle and what she had seen happen.

He touched her hair. "It's cool being here with you."

She smiled at him, but didn't say anything.

He started the car and they drove around for a while, but every street looked like every other street. Traffic was so dense that driving just a few miles felt like a road trip. The Kid had been to Los Angeles a few times, and he thought that driving on a street in Phoenix was like driving on a freeway in LA. "Where's downtown?" he asked Vanjii, thinking they could go there, park the car, get out and walk around.

Vanjii laughed, and when they drove downtown he understood why. There was nothing to explain why the district was known as "downtown." There were a few bars and restaurants, but there was nobody walking anywhere, and nowhere for them to walk to. People just parked their cars outside their destination and went inside.

"It ain't Santa Fe, huh?" said Vanjii.

They drove along Monroe Street, and the Kid noticed an Irish bar called McCaffrey's. It was five o'clock, and there was one vacant parking space across the street from the bar. The Kid took it as a sign.

As they walked towards the bar, the Kid saw that there was a hotel next door to it, called the San Carlos. It was one of the few buildings that looked as though it might have been around for a while.

"Hey, I got an idea," he said. "Instead of driving back tonight, let's stay at this hotel and go back in the morning."

"You paying?"

"Yeah."

They checked into the hotel, then went next door to McCaffrey's. The Kid liked the place; it was crowded and friendly, but not intrusive. Even though it was brightly lit, it somehow had an air of dark, rich warmth. They sat at a table and drank beer.

"Sorry I'm being so weird," Vanjii said to him.

"Weird? Shit, you just saw your uncle die. I ain't expecting you to party."

"It's not 'cause of my uncle. I could say it is, but it's not."

"Then what is it?"

" . . . You."

"What have I done?"

"I don't get you." She sat in silence for a moment, thinking he would ask her what she meant, but he didn't. "I just don't know why you're doing this shit."

"Doing what shit?"

"As soon as you met me, you took me to the hospital and took care of me. You only met me a few weeks ago. I mention that I want to go to Arizona and see my uncle, and right away you say you'll drive me . . . "

"So what's wrong with that?"

"There ain't nothing wrong with that. I just . . . Look, why are you so good to me?"

"I like you." He thought for a second and then smiled. "I *like you* like you."

Her eyes were huge in the lamplight of the bar. "Know something?" she said. "I love you."

Nobody had ever said it to him before, and he had never said it to anybody. He probably wouldn't have said it to her if she hadn't said it to him first, but now he said it and it didn't even feel weird. "I love you," he said.

They just sat there and looked at each other, and then the Kid smiled and said, "In fact, I *love you* love you."

Both of them laughing now, leaning across the table, their faces together, Vanjii's eyes wet and overflowing.

Later, they went to their hotel room. They were both quite drunk. The Kid watched Vanjii slip the straps of her blue dress off her shoulders, letting the dress fall from her body to make a pool at her feet, a pool she stepped out of. She was wearing white panties and no bra. She was already so wet from looking at the Kid, wanting him, that there was a spreading dark stain on the panties. He watched her take them off. She got in bed with him and they lay on their sides, holding each other and talking softly as they fucked for hours. When the Kid fell asleep, Vanjii lay close to him, watching his lips flutter with every breath he exhaled. She touched her face, feeling his dried come on her skin. She remembered her uncle looking up from the gurney.

NINE

The Kid and Miguel were drinking beer in the Cowgirl Hall of Fame. It was late in the evening and there was a blizzard outside. Their stomachs were full of food, and the beer in the bottles they were drinking from reflected the light just as it was meant to.

"I got to tell you something," said the Kid.

"I think I already guessed. Is it about Vanjii?"

"Yeah."

"Do I have to start saving for a wedding gift?"

"We ain't got that far. But we're gonna move in together."

Miguel smiled ruefully. "And I guess you ain't talking about her just moving into the house with us . . . "

"We're gonna get an apartment."

"Congratulations, you motherfucker. You get fucking domestic bliss, and I get to go back to eating in Denny's every night."

"I can teach you how to cook."

"Fuck you. I hope your dick drops off."

"What's a dick?"

Miguel stopped laughing. "Joking aside, bro . . . I'm happy for you. She's awesome. I hope it works out."

"Thanks."

"When you moving out?"

"Don't know yet. Soon as we find a place. Probably a couple months."

"God damn, I'm gonna miss you. You better have me over for dinner plenty."

— * —

The Kid hadn't had a job since high school. But now he knew he'd better start looking. He had about four thousand dollars left in the bank, and he knew it wouldn't carry him more than a few months. A friend of Vanjii's worked at a car dealership on the edge of town. He put in a word for the Kid, and got him a job as a receptionist there.

It was a no-brainer, the pay wasn't much, and he had to work six days a week, but the Kid liked it. All he had to do was sit behind the reception desk, answer the phone and transfer calls to the appropriate manager. He was supposed to greet potential customers when they came in, but he never had to because a salesman would grab them before they were all the way through the door. At first, the Kid enjoyed the novelty of having a job. When that wore off, he enjoyed the feeling of being paid to sit and read books between phone calls.

The Kid and Vanjii found an apartment on Cerrillos Road, near the barrio but not quite in it. It was a one-bedroom place in a large complex and was as cheap as they were going to find anywhere in town. It was populated mainly by couples and poor families, most of them Mexican, a few Indians and whites.

It was the first routine the Kid had had since high school, and he liked it. Waking up beside Vanjii in the cold and dark of morning, six or six-thirty, turning on the radio. Making breakfast for them both, then taking a shower, getting dressed and leaving. Driving on the freeway with all the other cars taking people to work, as the sky got lighter.

What he liked best was the evenings. Sometimes he'd go out with Miguel, or he and Vanjii would go out with Miguel and Maria, but more often he'd just stay home with Vanjii. He'd cook dinner and they'd lie around on the couch, watching movies or reruns of *The X-Files*. Later, they'd go to bed. Vanjii would go straight to sleep, but the Kid would read for a while. That was the best ever—in bed, reading a book, with Vanjii tucked in beside him, then getting drowsy and putting the book aside and turning the light off and falling asleep.

— * —

It was a Saturday morning. The Kid was sitting behind the reception desk, drinking a soda. It was the monsoon season, and the rain was so furious that there weren't many customers. The Kid had been reading, but the rain had distracted him, and now he was just staring at the glass door, watching the rain pound on it.

He saw something moving in the rain, something small and dark, coming close to the door and then moving away again. Then it came right up to the door and pressed against the glass. The Kid stood up, walked over and opened the door, and it ran past him and then mewled so loud it almost made him jump. It stood in front of his desk and looked at him, a tiny wet rag with a huge voice.

"What's up?" the Kid said.

The cat meowed urgently. Then it walked over to him and rubbed against his ankle.

"Uh . . . want some milk or something?"

The Kid bent and picked the cat up. It came to him easily and without fear, so he guessed it wasn't a stray. It didn't seem to be much more than a kitten. It hadn't fully grown into its ears. He couldn't tell how long it had been out in the rain—it was soaking, but the rain was heavy enough to have done that in a few minutes. He sat down and held the cat until it was warm, then put it on his desk and petted it. When it rolled onto its back, he looked closely and saw that it was male.

One of the sales guys, Chris, came over. "Got yourself a kitty?"

"Just found him outside. I don't know where he came from."

"What you gonna do with him?"

"Don't know. I'll see if somebody comes looking for him. Hey, can you get me some milk out of the fridge? I'd get it myself, but I don't want to leave him to run around."

"Sure." Chris went to the side room where the staff kept their snacks and came back with some milk in a saucer. He put it down on the floor by the Kid's desk. The Kid set the cat down by the saucer, and it went straight to it and started to drink. The Kid watched him. The rain continued to fall.

It was still raining when the Kid got off work. It was already dark. He drove slowly on the freeway, one hand on the steering wheel and the other hand petting the cat as it lay on the passenger seat. "You don't like driving, huh? Well, you're doin' good. Won't take much longer." When he got off the freeway he went to a mall. "I'll be right back," he told the cat. When it saw him start to get out of the car, it meowed in protest. "I swear, I'll be right back. Be cool, okay? Don't shit in my car."

He ran through the rain into the mall. There was a bookstore, and that was what he wanted. He bought a book about cats. Before leaving the mall, he went to the restroom to take a piss. There were three little kids in there, maybe seven or eight years old. One of them wanted to go into a cubicle to take a shit, but he was afraid his friends would leave while he did. "Bobby," said one of his friends. "Bobby. Can I ask you a question?"

"Yeah."

"Do you trust us?"

"Yeah."

"Then shut your motherfuckin' mouth."

The Kid didn't look at them. He pissed, washed his hands and ran back to his car.

— * —

He parked his car and hurried to his apartment, holding the cat inside his jacket to keep it warm and dry. He unlocked the door and went inside. Vanjii was lying on the couch, watching TV.

"Hey," she said. "What's that?"

"It's a cat. You know what those are, right . . . ?"

"Kiss my ass. Where'd you find it?"

"At work. His name's Catboy."

"How come?"

"Well, when I saw him, I realized he was a cat . . . "

"Whoa. You should go to college."

"And then I took a look at him and saw he wasn't a girl cat. So, Catboy. You got a better name?"

"No. C'mere, kitty."

The Kid lowered Catboy onto Vanjii's stomach. He purred and rubbed against her, marking her.

"You want to keep him?" she said.

"Well, yeah. Nobody showed up to claim him. I ain't gonna take him to the pound and let them kill him if nobody wants him. Looks like nobody wanted him already. I ain't gonna let that happen again. Besides . . . I want him."

"Uh-huh, he's cute. But we ain't allowed to have cats in the apartment."

"It's only not allowed if they catch you."

While the Kid cooked dinner, Vanjii went out and drove to a supermarket. She bought some cat litter and cat food. When she got home, she and the Kid constructed a makeshift litter tray out of a cardboard box lined with plastic. He said he'd go to a pet store and buy a real litter tray soon.

Catboy slept that night curled up on the Kid's chest. There was a huge windstorm that blew canopies of rain between the buildings of the apartment complex. Vanjii, of course, slept through it, but the Kid spent most of the night somewhere between waking and sleeping. He could hear the wind and rain all the time, and sometimes he could feel Catboy's claws on his chest, kneading. He dreamed that the wind was an old *bruja*, a witch, wandering the deserted streets outside, looking for Catboy so she could take him away and hurt him.

— * —

Sunday was the Kid's only day off work. Usually, he spent most of it in bed. He would wake up early, get up and make breakfast, then go back to bed. Vanjii would go out and get a newspaper, then bring it home, go into the bedroom and give it to the Kid. He would read it as he drank the coffee she brought him. Sometimes Vanjii would get in bed with him, and they would spend hours talking and fucking. Other times, she would go and meet friends or visit her father, and the Kid would stay there by himself, with newspaper sections spread over the blankets, listening to the mariachi music that blared from neighborhood houses when church was over. He'd get up and cook a late lunch at around three, then he and Vanjii might go see a movie.

That Sunday, though, he didn't read the paper. He read the book about cats he'd bought the day before. Vanjii lay in bed beside him, skimming through the paper. The Kid kept reading out loud to her.

"Hey, check this out. There's only one difference between regular cats and big cats, like lions and tigers. You know what the difference is?"

"Uh-uh."

"Size. Lions and tigers are just bigger. Besides that, they're just the same. The only reason Catboy doesn't try to eat us is we're bigger than him."

When Catboy meowed, Vanjii meowed back at him.

"You know what?" said the Kid. "Cats don't meow at each other."

"What do you mean?"

"I mean, they don't meow at each other. They got tons of different sounds they make to communicate with each other, but meowing ain't one of them. They only meow when they're trying to communicate with humans."

"How come?"

"Don't know. The book doesn't say."

"People don't meow, so where do cats get the idea from?"

"I don't know. Well, people do meow. You just meowed at him."

"Yeah, but I meowed back at him, dork. He did it first. And I already know cats meow."

"Yeah, well—maybe the first creature ever to meow was a human, and a cat heard it, and then told all the other cats that's the noise people make, so you better make it if you want humans to understand you . . ."

"You know something?" Vanjii kissed him. "If there was a National Weird Dude Directory, you'd get a five-star rating."

Later, the Kid got up and cooked chicken breasts with rice and a honey-and-lemon sauce. As he cooked, he listened to Elliott Smith. "I'm in love with the world/through the eyes of a girl/who's still around the morning after." He didn't know that Elliott Smith would stab himself to death with a knife.

— * —

Though he lived with them both, Catboy was always the Kid's cat. He didn't mind Vanjii, but he never seemed to like her much, except when she was the only one home when Catboy was hungry. He belonged to the Kid.

Catboy couldn't stand it when the Kid left for work in the morning, and you'd have thought he'd ingested catnip when the Kid came home in the evening. After cooking dinner, the Kid would lie on the couch in the living room, and Catboy would lie beside him, his cheek pressed against the Kid's.

To the Kid's regret, he had to ban Catboy from the bedroom. It was his only chance of getting a full night's sleep. Otherwise, he would be wakened by claws tearing his skin in affectionate kneading, or a rough tongue licking his head to show dominance. So, when the Kid and Vanjii went to bed, they'd close the door so Catboy couldn't get in. This was not taken lightly by Catboy. At first he tried aggression— he'd meow furiously outside the bedroom door, clawing at the carpet. When that got no response, he resorted to emotional blackmail. He had a collection of cat toys, his favorites being a spider the Kid had named Spidey and a mouse named Mickey. He'd try offering some of his toys to the Kid, leaving them by the bedroom door in a neat line. If Spidey and Mickey were among them, the Kid knew that Catboy had really been lonely for him.

It was the same routine every day when the Kid went to work. As soon as the Kid started to put his coat on, Catboy would stand by the front door of the apartment and wail. When the Kid got home that evening, Catboy would be all over him, purring, licking him and rubbing his head against him. The Kid had read that this wasn't the cuddling it seemed to be, it was marking with the cat's scent, but that was okay with him.

One night, Miguel was coming over for dinner. The Kid was roast-ing a chicken. Vanjii was taking a bath, soaking away the smell of the Woolworth's snack bar. The Kid went into the bathroom to take a piss. The bathroom light wasn't on. There was a little candle on the edge of the tub, and Vanjii was lying in the water, her eyes closed. She opened her eyes, looked at the Kid and smiled. "Hey," she said.

"Hey."

"How long till dinner?"

"A while. It's roasting. I can make you a snack if you're hungry."

"No, I'm okay. I just wondered how long I can lay here."

"Take your time." He bent over and kissed her.

After he'd pissed, he walked out of the bathroom and found Catboy snoozing on the hall carpet. Catboy raised his head, looked at the Kid and meowed. The apartment was full of the smell of roasting chicken.

The Kid wanted to stay there forever. He had a rush of feeling that if he and Vanjii and Catboy could just stay there in the small, dark apartment, with candles in the bathroom and a chicken cooking in the oven and the front door locked to keep the cold and all the bad things outside, then they would be all right and nothing would hurt them. For no reason he could understand, the Kid felt tears stinging his eyes.

— * —

The Kid loved supermarkets. It wasn't that he liked shopping for food, though he didn't mind it. What he loved was the feeling of being in a supermarket on a dark evening, the bright light of the store, and the people walking around the aisles, picking up the things they needed before going home. He imagined them later in the evening, cooking, eating, sitting on couches in living rooms, talking or watching TV. He never understood why this had such an effect on him, he just felt it and didn't question it. But he knew it had something to do with why his favorite TV show was the local news.

He loved sitting beside Vanjii, watching the news, hearing the anchor talk about what was happening in Santa Fe, seeing pictures of places he knew. Even if the news was bad, the Kid liked the feeling of watching it along with thousands of other people who lived there.

— * —

It was a Saturday night. Miguel had come over for dinner, and now the Kid, Vanjii, and Miguel were in Doctor Know. All three of them were quite drunk, though Miguel wasn't as bad as the others because he was driving. He had recently acquired a MOTHERS AGAINST DRUNK DRIVING bumper sticker, which he hoped would make it less likely that the cops would pull him over when he was driving drunk.

A group of young white women were sitting together at a table. One of them kept looking at the Kid. She was in her late twenties, thin, with lank blonde hair. At first the Kid thought she was checking him out, so he put an arm around Vanjii to give the woman the message, but she kept on staring. Then she began to cry. The Kid avoided looking at her when he saw that.

One of the woman's companions came over. "Hey," she said to the Kid. "My friend wants to talk to you."

"What about?"

"Her dad. Will you come and sit with us a minute?"

"Okay." He looked at Vanjii and Miguel. "I'll be right back."

"She hitting on you?" Vanjii said.

"No," the woman's friend said.

"Don't worry," said the Kid.

He went over to the other table. "Hey," he said to the woman. "What's up?"

She was still crying, but she had it under control and she wasn't sobbing. Tears were leaking silently out of her eyes and running down her face to merge with the snot that was coming out of her nose. She pulled her chair away from the table, out of earshot of her friends. "Are you the Kid?" she asked.

"Yeah."

"You don't know who I am, do you?"

"No."

She pulled another chair beside her. "Will you sit down? Just for a little while?"

He sat down.

"You killed my dad," she said.

"I think you got the wrong guy. I never killed anybody."

"You did. You shot him in the street outside of Evangelo's. His name was Tony Crowley."

The Kid didn't say anything.

"It's okay," she said, choking down sobs. "Well, it's not okay, but . . . I don't know. I just wanted to talk to you. I don't hate you or nothing. I don't know why I . . . It's just I wanted to talk to you."

"I didn't know your dad," the Kid said.

"I didn't either, not really . . . What did you kill him for?"

"He beat me up."

"I don't hate you. I just wanted to talk to you." She reached over and took the Kid's hand, squeezed it. The Kid squeezed back. "I just . . . I'm drunk," she said. "I'm sorry. I'm gonna leave."

"No, that's okay. I'll leave. Stay." He squeezed her hand again. "Sorry," he said. Then, for no reason he could make sense of, he said, "I'm drunk too."

When he looked at the woman, he tried to imagine that she could have come from Crowley, at least part of her, that she had been in him, in his balls, had sprayed out of his cock into her mother, that this was how she came into being. How Crowley came into being too. And Crowley was gone, destroyed, and she was there in the bar, and so was the Kid.

— * —

All he had to say to Miguel was, "Remember the biker? He was her dad." Miguel just nodded and muttered, "Jesus."

"What the fuck was that about?" Vanjii asked.

"I'll tell you when we get home," the Kid said.

Later, in bed, he asked her, "Do you really want to know?"

She thought about it and said, "No."

"But you know I've done stuff."

"Fuck, yeah. But it doesn't matter."

"It would matter to a lot of people."

"Yeah. Well, maybe they can afford it. But I can't. I don't know exactly what you've done. I know what people say, I know some of it must be for real. But I know you love me. And I'll take that where I can get it."

TEN

The Kid started baking chocolate macaroon cookies. He didn't have much of a sweet tooth himself, but Vanjii liked them, and he liked the process of making them. He found the recipe in a book, tried making some, and ended up making a batch just about every night. Vanjii couldn't eat them all and neither could he, so he'd usually put some of them in a Tupperware box, take them to work with him and share them with the sales people and customers.

The manager's name was Woody. He was a part-owner of the dealership. Each day he would show up at around ten in the morning, two hours after the Kid had started work. As he passed the reception desk, he would sometimes say hello to the Kid and sometimes ignore him. The Kid didn't mind either way. He didn't like Woody, and he didn't dislike him. If anyone had asked him what he thought of Woody, the Kid would have said he thought he was okay.

One morning, the Kid was talking to one of the sales guys. The guy was perched on the Kid's desk, and, as the two of them talked, they ate some of the cookies from the open box. Woody came in, said hello to them both, and took a cookie from the box. He walked away without saying anything else. The sales guy made an elaborate bow to him when his back was turned, but the Kid didn't smile.

When it was time for the Kid's lunch break, he went to Woody's office. "Hey," he said. "Can I talk to you for a minute?"

"Sure, if it's just a minute. I'm a little bit rushed . . ."

"You remember when you took one of my cookies this morning?"

Woody looked blank.

"When you came in this morning? I had a box of cookies on my desk, and you took one?"

Woody nodded. "Oh, yeah. I remember."

"Well, I think that was kind of rude. You didn't ask, you just took one. I mean, I bring them in here to share, I like people to eat them. But I don't like somebody just eating them without asking."

"Is it that big a deal?"

"It ain't the cookies, it's just you not asking. It's cool if you eat as many as you want, as long as you ask me. All the sales guys ask."

"I'm not one of the sales guys. I employ you."

"Yeah, but you don't employ me to make cookies."

"Okay. I apologize. I'll never touch your sacred fucking cookies again."

"You can, as long as you ask."

"Okay. Get back to work."

"I'm on my lunch break."

"Okay. Go and eat some lunch and let me work."

The next morning, the Kid was answering a phone call when Woody walked in. Woody waved a hand at the Kid and, as he walked by the reception desk, he took three cookies from the box and kept on walking.

"I'm sorry, I have to go," the Kid told the customer, and hung up the phone. He stood up. "Hey," he yelled after Woody. "Hey!"

Some sales people and customers stopped talking to each other and looked around. Woody stopped walking, turned and looked at the Kid. "Are you talking to me?"

"Yeah, I'm talking to you. Bring those back."

"Bring what back?"

"The cookies you took just now. They're mine. Bring them back."

Woody smiled, started to say something smart, then realized that the Kid was walking towards him. His smile disappeared. "What?" he said. "You going to fight me for some cookies?"

"If you want to," the Kid said. He reached Woody, stopped, held out his hand. "Give them to me."

"Are you threaten—?"

"They're mine. Give them to me."

Woody handed the cookies to the Kid. He started to say something, but the way the Kid was looking at him made him stop.

He went to his office and called the police.

The Kid was sitting at his desk when a cop walked in. "Is Mr. Lutgen here?" the cop asked.

"Yeah. I'll get him for you." The Kid picked up the phone, dialed Woody's extension, told him there was a police officer asking to see him. "He'll be right with you," the Kid told the cop.

Woody appeared about twenty seconds later. "I'd like you to take this guy out of here," he told the cop.

The cop looked at the Kid. "This guy?"

"Yeah, this guy. He threatened me with violence just before I called you."

"Then what's he doing sitting here working?"

"I didn't tell him he's fired. I don't know what he might do. I wanted to wait till you got here."

During this, the Kid said nothing.

"Did you threaten him?" the cop asked.

"No," said the Kid.

"He's a liar. I want him out of here," Woody said.

"Okay," the cop said to the Kid. "Whether you threatened him or not, he says you're fired. It'll save any trouble if you just leave."

The Kid nodded. He stood up, took his jacket from the back of the chair where it was hanging, put it on. He picked up the box of cookies from the desk, and walked towards the door.

"Don't come back here," Woody called after him. "I don't want you in this building. We'll send you your last check."

The Kid kept walking. He went out of the door and down the steps to the parking lot. He got in his car. The morning was cold and icy, and he had to let the engine idle for a minute. Then he drove out of the lot. As he paused at a corner, he looked once at the building. He had worked there, it had been good, and now he didn't work there anymore.

He wasn't sure where to go. It wasn't yet noon. Vanjii would be at work in the Woolworth's restaurant. He wasn't sure he wanted to go there and talk to her right now, but he didn't feel like being in the apartment either. He drove around for a while, just looking at the streets and houses and overcast sky. He ended up at the Cowgirl, eating a bowl of tortilla soup.

He felt as though he should think about what had happened, and what to do next, but he didn't know what to think, and he couldn't think of anything to do about it. He felt like he didn't know where he was. He wasn't where he had been, living with Miguel and selling drugs and doing favors for certain people, and he wasn't where he had been after that, working at the dealership six days a week. He was still with Vanjii, he knew that, but it felt like he was between places. It didn't even feel bad, it was more like he didn't feel anything, didn't know what he should feel.

When he'd finished his soup, he drove home. Catboy was glad to see him.

When Vanjii got home, the Kid was making a stir-fry. He told her what had happened.

"What an asshole. He called the cops on you?"

"Yeah. Guess he was too scared to just kick me out."

"Fuckhead." She came up behind him where he stood at the stove and put her arms around him. "What you gonna do?"

"Look for another job, I guess."

"What kind of a job?"

"Don't know. Same kind of job I was doing, probably."

That turned out not to be so easy. When the Kid applied for jobs, they would usual check with his last employer, and Woody would tell them what had happened, that the Kid was bad news. He managed to lie his way into a short series of jobs waiting tables, but he didn't last long at any of them. He was physically clumsy, and his memory wasn't methodical enough to keep track of different customers at different tables. He seemed to spend half the time apologizing to the tolerant customers, and the other half telling the intolerant ones to blow it out of their ass. And these jobs didn't make him enough money to live on. The job at the dealership hadn't paid a lot, but he worked so many hours that it added up. With the waiting jobs, it was impossible to get enough hours. It was manageable at first, because he still had a little money in the bank. But when that ran out, things got impossible. He and Vanjii were often late with the rent, which meant they had to pay late fees, which got them in even deeper.

One time, it all came together. They drove to the supermarket and spent the last of their money on food. The Kid's car ran out of gas just as he pulled into the apartment complex. And when they went into the apartment, they found that the electricity had been cut off.

Vanjii thought about calling her dad to see if he could lend her some money, but she knew he was broke and he'd already lent her too much. The Kid called Miguel, who said he'd come over right away with some cash. Then the Kid called the electric company and asked them to put the power back on. At first they refused, but the Kid said he was diabetic and needed the fridge to store his insulin. "If you don't turn it back on, you're gonna land me in the hospital," he said. When he promised to drive to their offices the next day and pay them, they gave in and the power came back on.

Vanjii went to bed early that night. The Kid stayed up late, stretched out on the living room couch, watching TV. He didn't know what to do. He thought about going back to the life, but there were two good reasons he didn't want to do that. One of them was in the bedroom, asleep after crying for a while. The other was sitting on the Kid's stomach, purring.

— * —

All you need is love, it says in a song. The song was written by a man who was rich, and it was probably true for him. But it wasn't true for Vanjii or the Kid. The love was there, but they stopped noticing it.

It was a Saturday afternoon, and Vanjii had suggested that they go to a movie. The Kid said okay. They were just about to leave when Vanjii counted what money they had and looked dubious. "You got any more money on you?" she asked.

"Yeah, I got about seven or eight bucks in my jacket."

"Give it to me."

He got the money from his jacket, which was hanging on a hook by the door. "Can we afford to go to the movie?" he said.

She ignored the question. "Give me the money."

"I asked you if we can afford to go to the movie. Answer me."

"I told you to give me the money. Give it to me."

The Kid threw the money at her. It hit her in the chest and fell to the floor. She picked it up, put it in her jeans pocket and walked out of the apartment without a word.

She drove to the theater and watched the movie by herself. When she got home, the Kid was reading a book. They didn't say anything to each other.

Vanjii went to bed, but she couldn't fall asleep. She got up and went into the living room. "Hey," she said to the Kid. "I was thinking about something."

"What?"

"You know the stuff you were doing before you met me? Maybe you should do something like that again."

The Kid didn't say anything, and he didn't look at her.

"Why not?" she said.

He still didn't look at her. "Because I don't want to be scared no more."

— * —

Vanjii moved out a week later.

ELEVEN

She went to Phoenix. She didn't tell the Kid where she was going, probably because she didn't know at the time she moved out. She wrote him a letter when she got there. He didn't write back, not because he was angry with her, but because he didn't know what to say.

He was sitting in the food court at the mall, reading her letter, when he felt someone looking at him. He looked up, at a young woman who was standing there with a baby in a stroller. She was smiling at him, and it took him a few seconds to recognize her.

"Hey, Lisa . . ."

"Hey yourself. How you doing?"

"Okay," he said, not wanting to tell her anything else. "How about you?"

"I'm good. I got married. And . . ." She motioned at the baby. "I got him."

"You still boxing?"

"Nah. I miss it, but you know . . . I gotta think about the baby. When he's ten, I don't want him having to tell his friends that the reason Mommy talks funny and drools on herself is 'cause she got whacked in the head too many times back when she used to be a boxer."

The Kid laughed. "Did you have many more fights since I saw you?"

"Hell, yeah. I won nine and lost four."

"Hey, you want to get some coffee or something?"

"Yeah, but I ain't got time. I just stopped in here quick to get something from Radio Shack. But it's good to see you."

"You too."

She grinned and ruffled his hair, then walked away, pushing the stroller.

The Kid walked out of the mall and got in his car. Before he started the car, he sat there and read Vanjii's letter yet again. It was only a page long. She said she hoped he was all right, and she said she was sorry for suggesting that he go back to the life. She was staying with a friend of a friend in Phoenix, and expected to be at that address for a while, if he wanted to write to her there.

He put the letter back in its envelope, and put the envelope in the glove compartment of the car. He thought about Lisa, what she was doing now, taking care of her baby. He thought about Miguel, and he didn't know what to think about himself.

TWELVE

The place Vanjii moved into was in an apartment complex on Phoenix's west side. There was a public phone in the street outside the complex, with a sign hanging above it that said, in Spanish, YOU CAN CALL MEXICO FROM HERE. There was nearly always someone using it. Most of the people in the complex had jobs, some had phones and some didn't, and none of them had any money.

Vanjii shared the place with two other people. Carlos, who'd been introduced to her by an old high school friend, had come to Phoenix from Santa Fe to learn to be an auto mechanic at a school there. He was hardly ever home. School and work kept him busy during the days and evenings, and he spent many of his nights at his girlfriend's place.

The other roommate was Louise. She was a native of the city, and had been doing well in her life until she'd suffered a head injury when a stranger stomped her for no reason that anybody knew of. Now she was frightened all the time, and never left the apartment unless she had to. She would often forget what she was talking about in the middle of a sentence. She worked part time as what she called a "telephone actress," talking dirty to men who called a phone sex company which patched the calls to her home number.

After paying her rent in advance, Vanjii had less than forty dollars. Her father had given her the money for the rent and the bus trip to Phoenix. She knew it wouldn't be hard to find a job, but she didn't have a car, and the bus service was a joke.

The apartment was on Seventeenth Avenue and Highland, about a mile away from Christown Mall. On her third day in Phoenix, Vanjii walked to the mall and talked a clothing store into hiring her.

The walk to work seemed dreamlike. Some of the streets had no sidewalks, so she walked in the gutter. Everything seemed too huge, fast and loud to be real. The cars blasted by her, the drivers sometimes yelling at her just because she was walking. The cars, and the life they contained, seemed far away from her, like a movie she was watching. She felt so tiny. The only other people she saw walking were homeless people, and they always came up to her and said the same thing. "Hey. Hey, I ain't panhandling. It's just that my car ran out of gas a couple miles away, and I lost my wallet, and my wife and kids are in the car, and . . ." Vanjii had nothing she could give them.

The heat didn't seem too bad while she was walking. But when she walked into the mall, with its air-conditioned chill, and sat down, the sweat came out so fast she felt like it was spurting out of her pores. She'd go into the restroom, take off her shirt and wipe herself down with paper towels, then put on some deodorant. She'd work all day, stopping to have lunch at one of the restaurants in the mall. When she walked back home, it would be getting dark and she'd be nervous, but she knew it wouldn't be long until she'd have saved a few hundred dollars, and she'd be able to buy a car.

There was a dumpster near the entrance to the complex, and a wooden post stood near it. Every day when Vanjii arrived home, she'd see a little girl playing tetherball—only she wasn't playing it with a ball, but with a plastic bag full of garbage she'd tied to the post. She always played by herself.

Vanjii wondered about the Kid, but it all seemed so far away that it didn't hurt as much as she'd thought it would.

— * —

The Kid was in a bar on Cerrillos Road, talking to a guy about maybe selling a little pot, something to make a little money in the short term, to keep eating and maybe pay next month's rent. It was about seven in the evening, and it was happy hour in the bar. The place was crowded, and the parking lot was full, so the Kid had parked in a small lot across the street. The lot was owned by a security firm, though the Kid didn't know that.

The Kid crossed the street in the darkness and walked into the lot. When he reached his car, he saw that it had been wheel-clamped.

He stood and looked at it for a moment, just not believing it. He got in the car and sat there, just taking it in. He spoke out loud, he said "Fuck!", and the word came out on a breath of laughter, but his face was wet with tears. He wiped his face with his hands, and sat breathing quietly, trying to get a hold of himself. Then he got out of the car and walked around the building, hoping that it was still open. It wasn't.

As he walked back to his car, he saw someone else walking through the lot, a white man in his early thirties. "Is this your car?" he asked the Kid.

"Yeah." The Kid pointed to the clamp. "I don't get this."

"I did it. I'm Dan Ward, I'm a partner in this company . . ."

"What company?"

He pointed at the building. "This company. We're a security patrol firm. This parking lot's private property."

"I didn't know . . . Sorry. I didn't see no sign."

"It should be obvious that this isn't public parking."

"Yeah. Sorry. I had to meet a guy in the bar over there, I couldn't find a place to park. I didn't see nobody here, so I thought it'd be okay."

"Well, you can see it's not."

"Can you take that thing off my car and I'll go?"

Ward nodded. "Sure. If you want to pay me your fine now."

"What?"

"There's a forty dollar fine for parking here."

"Bullshit. You can't do that. You can't just decide to fine somebody. You can tell me to get out of your parking lot, that's all."

"I'm not interested in a legal debate. I'm telling you there's a clamp on your car, and it's not coming off until you give me forty dollars."

"I don't have forty dollars."

"Uh-huh."

"Honest to God, I got about twenty, and I need that. It's all the money I got."

Ward looked at him and said nothing.

"Look, how about if I give you my address and you can . . ."

"Yeah, sure." Ward laughed. "How about if you come back here when you've got the money, and you can have your car back."

"Okay," said the Kid. "Okay. I'll give it to you now. Here . . ." He reached inside a pocket of his jacket.

When he had the knife out, the Kid swung it in a big circle, holding it with both hands, like someone swinging a baseball bat. It went into Ward's body with such force that the Kid felt the impact like a car hitting a wall. The Kid felt himself being thrown to the ground by the momentum, and he held on to the knife to steady himself, but it tore across Ward's lower abdomen and then slid out, and the Kid fell on his side. He jumped back up, still holding the knife, and saw that Ward was running away from him, letting out a noise that sounded like a donkey braying. Ward on made it a few steps, trying to ignore the things that were spilling out of him. But some of his intestines were trailing on the ground, and when he stepped on them his head seemed to shatter in a scream that never made it to his lips as he fell and the pain swallowed him.

The Kid stood over Ward, raised the knife, hammered it into his spine and left it there. Then he walked to the car, unlocked the door, got in. Blood was dripping from his hands. His body was shaking but he felt calm. He opened the glove box and took out some of the things that were in it—sunglasses, the letter from Vanjii, the Bulldog 44 he had used on Crowley. He put the sunglasses and letter in his jacket pocket, and stowed the gun in the waistband of his jeans.

He walked out of the parking lot into the street. As he walked, he felt his blood-soaked shirt chafing his skin. There was a 7-11 a couple blocks away. It had a phone outside. The Kid dropped two quarters into the phone and dialed Miguel's number.

He got the answering machine, and talked to it. "Hey, it's me. Something just happened . . . You'll probably hear about it. If you can, come and meet me tomorrow morning at the place where you hurt your ankle that time. Bring me some clothes. Come at around nine o'clock. If you don't want to, that's okay, I understand. Later."

He hung up the phone and walked away. After a few minutes he stopped, turned around, and walked back to the 7-11.

The guy behind the counter was named Randy. He was twenty-two. There were no other customers in the store when the Kid walked in, trembling, clothes bloody, blood in his hair, head swiveling, looking around the store.

"Hey, man, you okay?" Randy said. "You need an ambulance or something?"

The Kid pulled the Bulldog and pointed it at him. "Open the register. Give me the money. Don't touch an alarm or I'll fucking kill you."

"Please don't fucking kill me." Randy opened the register, started taking the cash from it and putting it on the counter.

"Hey! What the hell!"

The voice came from behind the Kid. He turned, saw a young woman who had come in the door and was now on her way back out. Her name was Laura, and her two-year-old daughter was outside in her car, fastened into the child restraint seat. The Kid pointed and fired. The sound of it concussed the air in the room. The bullet propelled Laura out the door, went in through her lower back, tore through her bladder and went out through her side. She lay on the asphalt and cried for her child as the life poured wet out of her.

"Please don't fucking kill me," Randy said again, but he was leaning over the counter, terrified, pawing at the gun in the Kid's hand. The Kid fired again, and most of Randy's face came apart.

The Kid pocketed all the bills from the register, and walked out of the store. He knew where he was walking to, but he didn't know if he would get there before a cop got him. It would depend on how long it took before somebody found the bodies at the 7-11, or the body at the parking lot. Even if that happened soon, he might still make it. He would have to elude the patrol cars, but there was a strong wind blowing, so there would probably be no police helicopters cruising tonight. But it was out of his control, so there was no use in worrying about it. Better just to keep walking, stick to the dark residential streets wherever he could, just keep walking, and either he would make it to Hyde Park or he wouldn't.

— * —

The stew was bubbling on the stove. Vanjii stirred it with a wooden spoon. It contained beef, carrots, tomatoes, and potatoes, and was seasoned with pepper, garlic, and cumin. The Kid had shown her how to make it.

Carlos was out with his girlfriend. Vanjii was going to share the stew with Louise, who was in the living room taking a phone call that had been forwarded by the sex line. Vanjii could hear her talking in a put-on, lisping, little-girl voice. "Yeah, honey, feel me contracting my ass around your cock . . . Oh, yeah . . ."

Vanjii stuck her head in the living room, looked at Louise and mouthed, "Contracting . . . ?" Louise grinned and shrugged. She had been watching TV when the call came, and she was still watching it, though she had muted the sound. The show was *Beavis and Butt-Head*.

— * —

Curled under a bush in Hyde Park, the Kid thought it would be funny if he froze to death during the night.

The place was a preserve of mountain and forest right there in the city. The Kid had made it there without seeing a cop and had spent an hour hiking up the mountain in the dark. He stopped near a spot where Miguel had sprained his ankle while walking with the Kid about a year earlier. He hoped Miguel would understand his message and show up there in the morning.

It was now around eleven. The Kid's intentions were simple. He was going to try to sleep and hope he didn't die in his sleep. When he woke, he was going to talk to Miguel, if Miguel showed. If Miguel didn't show, he would have to make another plan, but that was all he had right now.

He was shivering, huddled in his jacket, arms wrapped around himself. He could hear coyotes howling. He wondered if they would eat him if he died there. He wondered if he would be able to sleep in such cold, but as he wondered that, he felt the shivering stop and the drowsiness come. He knew that should frighten him; he had read somewhere that people who freeze to death feel like they're pleasantly falling asleep. He knew it should frighten him but it didn't. If this was a taste of the grave, it wasn't bad, it wasn't bad at all.

He fell asleep.

And when he woke up he was cold, but he was alive.

He looked at his watch. It was seven in the morning. He stood up, stretched, pissed. He wished he had a book to read, something to pass the time. He was still tired, but not tired enough to sleep any more, and too cold to keep still. He walked around in the woods, sometimes jogging a little, until he was warm. He wasn't hungry, but he was very thirsty.

He wondered if Miguel would come. He wondered why he had told him nine o'clock, rather than earlier or later. It had just come out of his mouth like that. Just before nine, he headed back to the spot where Miguel had fallen. He wondered if Miguel would remember exactly where it had happened.

Then he heard Miguel calling his name.

His first thought was that he shouldn't show himself, that Miguel might have been followed by the cops, or that they might have forced him to lead them to him. Then he told himself that Miguel would never do that to him, and there was no place for the cops to hide while they followed him up here.

"Hey," he yelled back. A second or two later, Miguel came in sight.

They stood there in the grass among the trees and looked at each other, Miguel in his suit and tie, the Kid in his bloody jeans and jacket.

"Jesus Christ, man," Miguel said.

"You hear what happened?"

"Yeah. I didn't know what the fuck you were talking about when I got your message last night, but it was on the news this morning. Three people, shit . . . Did you really do it?"

"Yeah."

"What for, bro?"

"I don't know."

"You don't know. You just kill three people but you don't know."

"One guy clamped my car . . ."

"Yeah, it said so on the news."

"And then I robbed the 7-11. But I really don't know."

"I don't even know what to say."

"Thanks for coming here."

"Fuck you. What am I supposed to do, just forget about you?"

"I didn't know if you would."

"That's because you don't know shit." Miguel started to cry.

"I need clothes," the Kid said.

"I brought you some, like you asked. They're in my car. Wait here and I'll get them." Miguel walked to the road, got a backpack from his car, walked back into the woods. The Kid was now sitting on the ground. Miguel dropped the backpack in front of him.

"Thanks," the Kid said.

"You better head for Mexico. There's no way you can beat this. They got you on video at the 7-11, and they got a body laying next to your car. White people. You're looking at death row for sure."

The Kid didn't say anything.

"Get to Mexico. You can just disappear there, they'll never find you. The narcos'll cover your ass if you work for them. But go. You gotta go."

"I know. I'm gonna go."

"How?"

"I'll steal a car."

"You know how to hot-wire?"

"No."

"You gonna kill somebody to get a car?"

"I don't know. Maybe."

Miguel was crying hard. He took out his car keys and threw them at the Kid. "Asshole. Asshole. Take my fucking car."

"Miguel . . ."

"Shut up. Take the fucking car. I'm still paying it off, so I guess insurance'll cover it, maybe. I'll wait a couple days before I report it stolen. At least you won't get pulled over driving a hot car."

"Thanks. You know the cops'll probably figure it out that you helped me."

"Fuck them. They got to prove it." Miguel sat down on the ground beside the Kid. "Asshole. What happened? I thought I was gonna be best man at your wedding for sure."

"You would've been."

"I know. And you would've been my best man. Oh my God. My God."

They sat there together for a few minutes, not looking at each other and not saying anything. Miguel stopped crying, wiped his face with his tie. Then the Kid said, "Hey, Miguel?"

"What?"

"Listen, it's gonna be all right. I'm gonna be all right."

"Sure you are."

"No, I mean it. I don't want you to be worried. I don't want you to worry about anything. It'll be all right."

Miguel stood up, and then the Kid did the same. The Kid held out a dirty, bloodstained hand, and Miguel took it and squeezed it. "You gonna be in touch sometime?" Miguel asked. "At least let me know you made it?"

"Don't worry about anything."

"You got money?"

"Yeah."

"Shit. You got it from the 7-11."

Miguel walked away. He didn't look back.

The Kid opened the backpack and searched inside it. There were two pairs of jeans, two T-shirts, a thick shirt, a wool jacket, boxer shorts, socks, a pair of running shoes. He stripped off his own clothes, the cold making his teeth chatter, and put on Miguel's. The shoes were a little bit too big, but they would do. He spat several times on the shirt he had taken off, and used it to wipe his hands and face. He bundled his discarded clothes together and hid them under a bush. Then he picked up the backpack and walked to the road.

Miguel's car was a white Camaro. The Kid got in and looked at himself in the rearview. There was still some dried blood on his face and in his hair. He licked his fingers and rubbed it off his face, then ran his fingers through his hair, brushing the red flakes away. Then he put on his sunglasses and started the car.

As he drove down the road into the city, he saw Miguel, who was walking quickly. As he drove past him he honked the car horn, and Miguel waved a little. The Kid watched him in the rearview until he couldn't see him anymore.

— * —

Driving the car was strange at first. It was hard to figure out how the lights, the locks, all these things, worked. But after he'd driven it for an hour, it was so familiar that he felt like it was his.

He wanted to go and get Catboy, but he knew he couldn't. The cops might be watching the apartment, and, even if they weren't, they would certainly have forced their way in by now. They would either have taken Catboy to the pound or just ignored him, in which case he would be on the street again. The Kid fought a temptation to drive around and look for him.

He knew he'd better get out of town right away. At first he thought that the cops would think he'd left by now, so it might be safer to stay put and hide. But where would he hide? Too many people knew what he looked like and might call the cops as soon as they saw him. He knew there would be many vatos getting pulled in for questioning and fingerprinting on the off-chance that they might be him. Once he was far away from Santa Fe and Albuquerque he'd be safer, and safer still when he was out of the state. They'd be looking for him to head for Mexico, but that was okay with him because he wasn't going to Mexico. At least not yet.

He drove at the speed limit to Albuquerque. The car had a quarter tank of gas left. He wondered whether it would be safer to stop at a busy gas station there in town where he might be recognized but probably wouldn't be noticed, or in a quiet one outside of town where he was less likely to be recognized but more like to be noticed and remembered. Somehow it felt as though a gas station in town would be safer, but he just didn't want to get out of the car, so he got on the I-40 going West, and filled up with gas at a place about ten miles out of the city.

THIRTEEN

Twice he saw cop cars on the highway and waited for the flashing lights to come on, but nothing happened. He kept going for a few hours, not stopping until he reached Gallup. He got some gas there and picked up some food at a drive-through fried chicken place. Back on the highway, he steered with one hand and used the other to eat. It was starting to get dark, and somehow that made him feel safer.

The highway was busy. There were signs instructing slower traffic to stay in the right lane, which he did. He gazed at the barriers at the side of the road, and wondered about the men who had placed them there, the men who had built the road. He wondered how many men it had taken, how they had done it, how much they got paid, what they were doing now. He wondered if they liked building the road and what it felt like to them when they drove on it. He didn't know why he wanted to know about them, because he had never wondered about them before.

He kept thinking about his apartment, about the things it contained, his cooking equipment, Catboy. His life with Vanjii. He wished he had asked Miguel to take care of Catboy.

In the early evening, he crossed the Arizona state line. When he reached Flagstaff, he got on the I-17 and headed south, until the pines gave way to cactus.

— * —

When Vanjii got home from work, she was pleased to see that the little girl who played tetherball had gotten a real ball. Because she had a ball, she now had friends, two other girls were playing with her. Vanjii smiled at them as she walked past, but they didn't pay her any notice.

Louise told her that her dad had called twice. Vanjii called him back, and he told her what he had seen on TV. Vanjii yelled at him, then she said she was sorry. She hung up. Then she looked for

Miguel's number, called it and talked to him. Miguel didn't want to talk, because he was afraid his phone might be tapped. He didn't tell Vanjii that, he just said he had to go out somewhere. She was angry with him, but he called her from a public phone about ten minutes later and they talked for a long time.

— * —

It was around eight in the evening when the Kid reached Phoenix. He was aiming for downtown, but he lost his bearings and ended up driving east. He passed Tempe, then Guadalupe, though he didn't see Guadalupe because a mile-long wall had been built by the freeway so that drivers wouldn't have to look at how the people there lived. When the Kid saw the exit for Ahwatukee, he knew for sure he was going the wrong way, so he pulled off the freeway, intending to turn around.

He saw a strip mall along the street and realized that he was very hungry. He drove into the mall and saw that there were a few restaurants. He parked the car and got out. The heat of the night hit him as soon as he stepped out of the car's air conditioning.

There was a Japanese place called Sakana. There were no unoccupied tables, so he went and sat at the sushi bar. He'd never tried sushi before. He ordered smoked salmon, eel, and a spicy tuna hand roll. He sat there and drank a beer and watched the sushi chefs prepare the food. He had never seen anything like it before, how fast and fluid their movements were, chopping and rolling and folding. He wanted to ask them where he could learn to do that, but he didn't.

When his food arrived, it seemed like the best thing he had ever eaten. He paid for it and left.

He headed back into Phoenix. He exited on Seventh Street, went along to Monroe and drove west a few blocks, until he saw McCaffrey's, the pub he and Vanjii had once gone to, adjacent to the hotel they had spent the night in. He found a parking space down the street, parked and walked to the bar.

It was busy. There were people who'd come for happy hour and never managed to leave, and people just arriving after movies or the hockey game at America West Arena. At one end of the bar, a band was playing folk songs. The Kid ordered a beer and sat at the bar and listened to the band.

At the beginning of a song, a woman and a man got up and started to dance, standing right in front of the musicians. They danced slowly, holding each other close. The man was balding and the woman had gray in her hair and the Kid somehow knew they had been together for years. It felt like a knife in his spine.

When the band took a break, he pulled Vanjii's letter from his pocket, looked at the phone number, and dialed it on the bar's public phone. It rang busy. He tried again just before the bar closed, but it was still busy.

— * —

Louise was in the living room, working the phone, talking to men as they jacked off. Carlos, as usual, wasn't home. Vanjii was in the kitchen, drinking coffee and staring at the table. She hadn't told Louise anything and didn't think she was going to. She didn't even know how to tell it to herself.

A fly landed on the table. It sat there, eyes sending images to the brain, lungs receiving oxygen, heart beating with certainty. Vanjii didn't think, she just slapped with her hand, coming from behind so the fly saw nothing, and then the fly was crushed flat, just a stain on the wood. Vanjii washed her hands and made more coffee. She wondered when she'd be able to cry.

— * —

When the Kid left the bar, he walked around for a few minutes. At one in the morning, it felt hardly less warm than a summer afternoon in Santa Fe. The downtown streets were so clean they looked sterile, and a person slept in every other doorway. The Kid wanted to walk for longer, but he could find nowhere to walk to, so he went to his car.

He was almost out of gas. He stopped at a Circle K on First Avenue and Van Buren. As he was pumping the gas, a guy came up to him. "Hey. Excuse me . . ."

The Kid looked at him and didn't say anything.

"Listen," the guy said. "I real need a favor. My little girl's sick, and she's at Thirty-Fifth Avenue and Camelback, and I need to go there and see her tonight, but I got no car. If you can just give me a ride up there, I'll give you five bucks for the gas."

The Kid didn't question the guy's story, because he could see right through it. The reason the story wasn't more credible or better explained was because the guy was junk sick, and he wanted to go visit his dealer.

"I been asking lots of people, and they all said no. I really need to see her, man."

"Okay," said the Kid. "I'll take you there, but I ain't got time to wait for you and bring you back."

"That's okay, that's no problem. I just need you to take me there. Thank you."

The drive took about fifteen minutes. The junkie clumsily tried to make conversation, and the Kid went along with it. "Okay, right here," the junkie said, pointing to an apartment complex. The Kid slowed down, and the junkie got out. "Thanks a lot, man," he said to the Kid. "Really."

"Sure," said the Kid. The junkie tried to pay him for the gas, but the Kid shook his head and drove away.

That junkie was me. It was the only time I ever met the Kid. And it was the first time in years that anybody had helped me out when they didn't have to. I don't know why he did it, I just know he did.

The neighborhood was nicknamed "Gangs R Us," and the cops were going there more and more often, trying to show a presence. As the Kid drove away, he passed a cop car waiting at a corner. When the cop saw the New Mexico plates, he thought the Kid might either be a visitor who'd gotten lost and could use some advice on neighborhoods to stay out of, or else a drug dealer doing some interstate networking. Either way, the cop felt like talking to him, so he fell in behind him and turned on his lights.

When the Kid saw the lights, the panic rose up inside him like vomit, and he fought to control it and decide what to do. He knew Miguel hadn't reported the car stolen yet, so unless the cops had some-how found out, that couldn't be it. But even if it was just that he had a light out or something, the cop would ask to see a driver's license.

The Kid pulled over and turned off the engine. He watched the cop get out of the car and walk towards him. When the cop was near at his window, the Kid started the car and took off, as the cop sprinted back to his car.

The Kid turned a corner, hit the brakes, jumped out of the car and ran. He heard the cop car appear behind him. He ran harder, shrieking air into his lungs, looking for cover, a place to hide. There wasn't any.

"Hey, asshole. Stop right now or I'll shoot."

The Kid stopped. Raised his hands. Turned around.

The cop had gotten out of his car and was pointing his gun at him. "Lie down and put your hands behind your back."

The concrete warm against his cheek. The handcuffs closing around his wrists.

FOURTEEN

Madison Street Jail was only a short distance from the pub where he'd spent the evening. The Kid was booked in and fingerprinted and put in a cell.

It was known as the Horseshoe, and it was like no jail the Kid had ever heard of. People would be rotated from cell to cell, so that they lost track of time. The cells they put him in were completely covered with men. There were men sleeping curled around the toilet that had shit dripping off the sides and piss all around the floor. Men were sleeping on top of other men. Others were using toilet rolls as pillows. They lay on the trash that was scattered everywhere from the sack lunches that were provided. The smell was like a kick in the face by a dirty foot.

No one is sure how long the Kid stayed there, but it wasn't very long.

— * —

Jeremy Ruvin should have been a cop. He loved cops, and cops loved him. Like many veteran cops, he was a legend in his own lunchtime. But Ruvin wasn't a cop. He was a reporter.

He had spent twenty years at the *Phoenix Weekly*, a free sheet that was distributed throughout the city. It was part of a national chain of weekly papers, and it regarded itself as the only real news outlet in the Valley. This wasn't much of a boast; Phoenix was a city without a real newspaper. The main daily, the *Arizona Republic*, was almost devoid of news and existed to further the interests of the corporations that were developing the city. Its rival, the *Tribune*, had a publisher who openly supported the banning of reporters—including the paper's own—from government meetings to discuss whether public money should be given to aid corporate development. A famous local swindler once observed that, in Phoenix, when you try to sell people out, they take the first offer.

The *Phoenix Weekly* was a tabloid full of long, turgid stories that few people read. But Ruvin's stories won Arizona Press Club awards every year, and had done for as long as anyone could remember. Although his stories were as slanted as those of his peers, they were packed with lurid detail. The cops gave him access that they gave to no one else. Because, no matter what the facts might be, Ruvin would make them look good.

This was something they needed. Phoenix was among the leaders of the country when it came to unjustified police shootings. The city had to pay out millions in lawsuits, and more were pending. But, in the world of Ruvin, every cop on the force was a heroic figure who only shot or beat up unarmed civilians when it was strictly necessary. He never actually lied in print; he just stayed away from stories that might show the police department as it really was.

Ruvin had few hobbies. The only thing he cared about was his identity as a reporter, and the only people he hung out with were the cops and prosecutors he wrote about. In his mind he was famous, his world a black and white movie in which he wore a raincoat and fedora with a tag that read PRESS and talked out of the side of his mouth. He imagined the raincoat and fedora so vividly that when you were in his presence you felt like you could almost see them.

When the cops realized that they had the Kid, then realized that they didn't have him anymore, the first reporter they called was Ruvin.

Ruvin and Detective Zack Blantyre had been friends for years. Blantyre had asked Ruvin to write a biography of him, and Ruvin had been sporadically working on it. Now they sat in Durant's restaurant on Central Avenue, and Ruvin asked Blantyre what had happened.

"We don't know what happened," Blantyre said.

"Zack. You find out you have a triple murderer in your jail. Then you find out he's not in your jail anymore. And you're telling me nobody knows what happened?"

"Okay, off the record—for now, okay . . ."

Ruvin nodded.

"We do know. He just walked out of there, him and four others. Somebody forgot to lock a door, and five of them just walked. We know it happened, we just don't know how it happened."

"Zack, no matter how I say it, you know that's not going to look good."

"No shit. No shit. I mean, it's not like it's the first time this kind of crap's happened at the jail . . . But a fucking three-time killer. You know as well as I do, most of the guys in there are there because they're fucked in the head and got no money . . . but you get guys like this sometimes. I've been saying for a long time that something like this was gonna happen down there someday if they didn't start hiring people who know which way is up."

"He's from New Mexico?"

"Yeah."

"So what did he come here for?"

"How should I know, Jer? While we're asking stuff, what did he kill three people for?"

"I'll sit on this," Ruvin said. "But I can't for long."

"I'm not asking you to. I just wanted to let you know about it first."

"Appreciated. Look, I'm not gonna wait and eat lunch. I'll get something on the run. I'm gonna head out to New Mexico today."

— * —

The Kid didn't expect it to work, but when the other guys started to walk out, he followed them. And when nobody stopped them, they kept walking. And when they were outside on Madison Street in the sunshine, and the cops who were entering the building ignored them, they split up and kept walking.

— * —

Miguel was in his pajamas, eating toast for breakfast when the cops knocked on his door. He let them in, and they asked him about the Kid and he lied. Then they asked him where his car was, and he knew he was fucked. They let him get dressed before they put the handcuffs on him.

— * —

The Kid knocked on the door. Vanjii opened it. She was wearing shorts and a T-shirt with the name of the store she worked for on it. She had been getting ready to walk to her job.

Her first impulse was to close the door, but the Kid pushed it open with his foot and stepped into the apartment. They stood there in the living room looking at each other.

"You gonna kill me?" Vanjii said, her voice breaking.

"What?"

She began to sob. "I don't want to die."

"What would I kill you for? Why would I do that?"

"You killed those other people . . . I don't know . . ."

"You think I would hurt you? You're scared of me?"

" . . . Yeah." She looked so small, her face crumpled, tears and snot everywhere.

"You said you knew I loved you and you'd take that where you could get it . . ."

He reached out to touch her. She was too frightened to pull away, so she closed her eyes and cringed violently when he put his hand on her shoulder.

Louise came out of her bedroom "Vanj? What's wrong? You okay?"

The Kid turned like an animal and ran.

— * —

He walked, not trying to hide himself, not trying to stop the sun from burning him. He walked along Camelback until he reached Seventh Avenue, and then he walked south to Encanto Park. It was only a few miles, a walk that would have meant nothing to him in Santa Fe, but the heat of Phoenix made it seem like he was wading through hot water. When he reached the park, his head was spinning and his mouth was as dry as the ground.

He lay down in the shade of a tree and kept still until his vision came into focus. Then he walked around, looking for someplace to get water. The cops had taken all his money. He went up to people and asked them if they'd buy him some water, and one guy gave him a couple dollars and told him there was a vendor at the children's play area, Encanto Kiddie Land. He went there and bought a bottle of water and then went and lay down under another tree and drank it all.

He remembered how Vanjii had looked when she'd cried. He didn't know it, but his own face now looked like hers had, twisted like it might come apart, bawling, snorting, so frightened. He couldn't believe he hadn't known she would be afraid of him. Who wouldn't be afraid of him? He thought about the life he always pretended to himself that he had: cooking, listening to music, driving his car, reading books, talking to his friends, falling in love with Vanjii, taking care of his cat. And he thought about the life he really had: people scared, people hurt, people dead.

He thought about what he had once said to Vanjii. I don't want to be scared no more.

— * —

Vanjii was sitting on the couch and Louise was holding her while she cried. She kept trying to explain what had happened, but Louise's head condition made it hard for her to follow because she couldn't remember things. She just kept stroking Vanjii's hair and saying, "It's okay. Nobody's gonna hurt you."

— * —

Ruvin didn't have to spend long in Santa Fe. He talked to the cops and asked if they'd let him talk to Miguel, but they weren't Phoenix cops so they wouldn't. Then he walked around the barrio, knocking on doors. Some people told him the Kid didn't exist, that he was just a ghost, a legend, a scary story for late at night. Other people gave him names and addresses. He was soon talking to the Kid's mother. She didn't have much to tell him in terms of facts, but she gave him plenty of color he could use in his story. About an hour later, he was sitting in a living room talking to Vanjii's father.

As soon as Ruvin left that apartment, he pulled out his cell phone and called Blantyre. He got voice mail. "Zack, it's Jerry. I'm in Santa Fe. Listen up, I've got an address for you . . . " He recited the address twice. "It's the address of the Kid's girlfriend. They used to live together, and she moved to Phoenix a few weeks ago. He must have gone there to see her. I'm just gonna head to Albuquerque and fly home, so do me a favor—don't do anything until I get there, okay?"

He put the phone away and got in his rental car.

— * —

The Kid lay there on the ground for most of the day, sleeping on and off. He stayed there after the park closed and it got dark. Then he got up and started to walk. It was hard to move. Each step hurt. He knew he needed more water, but he wasn't going to ask anyone for money, and he wasn't going to hurt anyone for it. He walked for two hours, falling a few times, always getting up and walking on.

— * —

The apartment door seemed to explode as the cops forced it open. Vanjii, Louise, and Carlos were in the living room, and when the cops saw Carlos they pointed their guns at him and screamed for him to get down on the floor. Vanjii and Louise screamed back at them. From a safe distance, Ruvin took notes.

— * —

The Kid couldn't walk any more, and he'd never known where he was walking to anyway. He was very close to the apartment Vanjii had lived in as a child, but he didn't remember that and he hadn't gone there on purpose. He saw a public phone outside a liquor store, went to it, fumbled in his pocket for the change he had left after buying the water in the park. The call would cost fifty-five cents, and he knew he had a little more than that. He found it and fed it into the machine and dialed.

"Hello?" said Vanjii.

"It's me. Listen, I'm sorry I scared you. I don't want you to be scared . . ."

"Okay," she said, and he heard it in her voice.

"The cops are there, huh?"

"Yeah."

"I'm so sorry, honey."

"I know. I am too." Pause. "You don't sound good."

"Don't worry. Can I talk to the cops?"

"What're you gonna do?"

"I'm just gonna keep on loving you, that's what. That's the only thing I can do. And nobody's gonna get hurt no more. You don't need to be scared no more."

She said something to someone else. He couldn't hear what it was. Then a voice said, "This is Detective Blantyre."

"Yeah, hey, bitch. Fucking listen. Here's where I'm at—Fifteenth Avenue and Grand. There's a lot across the street from the liquor store. I'll be waiting for you there."

"What are . . . ?"

"Shut your fucking hole. Come on down here so I can kill your white ass." The Kid hung up. Very slowly, he walked across the street to the empty lot, and sat on the ground.

Vanjii. Vanjii. Vanjii. I'm so scared. I love you and love you and I'm so scared.

A homeless guy wandered into the lot. He came over and tried to talk. "You better get out of here," the Kid told him. "The cops are coming. It's gonna be bad."

The guy didn't believe him, thinking he just wanted to have the lot to himself. But then he heard the sirens and knew it was true, and he ran.

There were six cars. The Kid was sitting with his back to the wall, and the cops stood behind the cars, forming a semicircle around him. They all had guns aimed at him.

Vanjii. Vanjii. He kept bringing her face into his mind, remembered how she looked when she was smiling in the bathtub in candlelight and loving him.

"Lie down on the ground and put your hands on top of your head! Do it right now!"

He stood up, flipped them off with one hand, and reached in his pocket with the other, pretending he was reaching for a gun. He didn't get his hand out of the pocket before the bullets hit him, turning him weightless and throwing him against the wall. It hurt and it didn't hurt and then it hurt again. The cops kept on firing until there were bullet holes even in the soles of his feet, but he didn't know that. He thought about Catboy and hoped that nobody would be mean to him.

— * —

Then he was dead, and some people cried, but most didn't. And the people with lawns and 401(k) plans and straight white teeth felt safer now, because the Kid was gone. But, in hospitals and houses in the barrios, more kids were being born. And, when they were born, they were slapped on the ass and they started to cry. With their first breath they started to cry, and they would not be quiet because they knew what was theirs.

ACKNOWLEDGMENTS

I've heard it said many times that writing is a lonely occupation. This is not true if the writer has friends like mine.

Years ago, on a cold winter night in Santa Fe, Chrissie Orr and I were eating, drinking, and talking as we sat together in the warmth of the Cowgirl Hall of Fame, and the idea for this novel came to me during our conversation. I told Chrissie, who then encouraged me to write it. I am grateful to her, for that and many other things.

There are people to whom I owe thanks who would prefer not to be mentioned by name, some for reasons of good taste and some because they have cases pending. My gratitude to them is no less because they are anonymous.

Thanks also: Larry Fondation, Nick Hentoff, Cecily Dubusker, Taryn Shell, Craig Taylor, Dale Baich, M.V. Moorhead, Chuck Bowden, Lonna Kelley, Rebecca Story, Susan Thompson, Rebecca Hoelting, Daishin Bree Stephenson.

And to Andrea Gibbons and Gary Phillips, without whom you wouldn't be reading this book right now.

A sliver of this book appeared, in different form, in the anthology *Phoenix Noir*. I'm grateful to Patrick Millikin for that.

A man can live and write without cats, but why would he? Nine deep bows to Jimmy and Maggie, who taught me that opposable thumbs don't mean I'm smart.

BG
The Sitting Frog Zen Center
Phoenix, Arizona
Summer, Year of the Tiger

ABOUT THE AUTHOR

Barry Graham is a fiction writer, poet, journalist, and blogger whose novels have received international acclaim and whose reporting has helped more than one corrupt politician leave office.

Born and dragged up in Glasgow, Scotland, he has traveled widely and has been based in the United States since 1995. His previous occupations include boxing and grave-digging. He is also a Zen monk and serves as the Abbot of The Sitting Frog Zen Center in Phoenix. He has witnessed two executions, invited by the inmates, not the state. To keep up with what he's doing, find him online at dogobarrygraham.net.

PM PRESS was founded at the end of 2007 by a small collection of folks with decades of publishing, media, and organizing experience. PM Press co-conspirators have published and distributed hundreds of books, pamphlets, CDs, and DVDs. Members of PM have founded enduring book fairs, spearheaded victorious tenant organizing campaigns, and worked closely with bookstores, academic conferences, and even rock bands to deliver political and challenging ideas to all walks of life. We're old enough to know what we're doing and young enough to know what's at stake.

We seek to create radical and stimulating fiction and non-fiction books, pamphlets, t-shirts, visual and audio materials to entertain, educate and inspire you. We aim to distribute these through every available channel with every available technology — whether that means you are seeing anarchist classics at our bookfair stalls; reading our latest vegan cookbook at the café; downloading geeky fiction e-books; or digging new music and timely videos from our website.

PM Press is always on the lookout for talented and skilled volunteers, artists, activists and writers to work with. If you have a great idea for a project or can contribute in some way, please get in touch.

PM Press • PO Box 23912 • Oakland, CA 94623
www.pmpress.org

Friends of PM Press

These are indisputably momentous times — the financial system is melting down globally and the Empire is stumbling. Now more than ever there is a vital need for radical ideas.

In the three years since its founding — and on a mere shoestring — PM Press has risen to the formidable challenge of publishing and distributing knowledge and entertainment for the struggles ahead. With over 100 releases to date, we have published an impressive and stimulating array of literature, art, music, politics, and culture. Using every available medium, we've succeeded in connecting those hungry for ideas and information to those putting them into practice.

Friends of PM allows you to directly help impact, amplify, and revitalize the discourse and actions of radical writers, filmmakers, and artists. It provides us with a stable foundation from which we can build upon our early successes and provides a much-needed subsidy for the materials that can't necessarily pay their own way. You can help make that happen—and receive every new title automatically delivered to your door once a month—by joining as a Friend of PM Press. And, we'll throw in a free T-Shirt when you sign up.

Here are your options:

- **$25 a month** Get all books and pamphlets plus 50% discount on all webstore purchases

- **$25 a month** Get all CDs and DVDs plus 50% discount on all webstore purchases

- **$40 a month** Get all PM Press releases plus 50% discount on all webstore purchases

- **$100 a month Superstar** — Everything plus PM merchandise, free downloads, and 50% discount on all webstore purchases

For those who can't afford $25 or more a month, we're introducing Sustainer Rates at $15, $10 and $5. Sustainers get a free PM Press T-shirt and a 50% discount on all purchases from our website.

Your Visa or Mastercard will be billed once a month, until you tell us to stop. Or until our efforts succeed in bringing the revolution around. Or the financial meltdown of Capital makes plastic redundant. Whichever comes first.

Send My Love and a Molotov Cocktail: Stories of Crime, Love and Rebellion

Edited by Gary Phillips and Andrea Gibbons

ISBN: 978-1-60486-096-2
256 pages $15.95

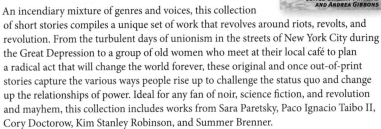

An incendiary mixture of genres and voices, this collection of short stories compiles a unique set of work that revolves around riots, revolts, and revolution. From the turbulent days of unionism in the streets of New York City during the Great Depression to a group of old women who meet at their local café to plan a radical act that will change the world forever, these original and once out-of-print stories capture the various ways people rise up to challenge the status quo and change up the relationships of power. Ideal for any fan of noir, science fiction, and revolution and mayhem, this collection includes works from Sara Paretsky, Paco Ignacio Taibo II, Cory Doctorow, Kim Stanley Robinson, and Summer Brenner.

Full list of contributors:

Summer Brenner	Cory Doctorow
Rick Dakan	Andrea Gibbons
Barry Graham	John A. Imani
Penny Mickelbury	Sarah Paretsky
Gary Phillips	Kim Stanley Robinson
Luis Rodriguez	Paco Ignacio Taibo II
Benjamin Whitmer	Ken Wishnia
Michael Moorcock	Michael Skeet
Larry Fondation	Tim Wohlforth

The Chieu Hoi Saloon
Michael Harris

ISBN: 978-1-60486-112-9
376 pages $19.95

It's 1992 and three people's lives are about to collide against the flaming backdrop of the Rodney King riots in Los Angeles. Vietnam vet Harry Hudson is a journalist fleeing his past: the war, a failed marriage, and a fear-ridden childhood. Rootless, he stutters, wrestles with depression, and is aware he's passed the point at which victim becomes victimizer. He explores the city's lowest dives, the only places where he feels at home. He meets Mama Thuy, a Vietnamese woman struggling to run a Navy bar in a tough Long Beach neighborhood, and Kelly Crenshaw, an African-American prostitute whose husband is in prison. They give Harry insight that maybe he can do something to change his fate in a gripping story that is both a character study and thriller.

"Mike Harris' novel has all the brave force and arresting power of Celine and Dostoevsky in its descent into the depths of human anguish and that peculiar gallantry of the moral soul that is caught up in irrational self-punishment at its own failings. Yet Harris manages an amazing and transforming affirmation—the novel floats above all its pain on pure delight in the variety of the human condition. It is a story of those sainted souls who live in bars, retreating from defeat but rendered with such vividness and sensitivity that it is impossible not to care deeply about these figures from our own waking dreams. In an age less obsessed by sentimentality and mawkish 'uplift,' this book would be studied and celebrated and emulated." — John Shannon, author of *The Taking of the Waters* and the Jack Liffey mysteries

"Michael Harris is a realist with a realist's unflinching eye for the hard truths of contemporary times. Yet in *The Chieu Hoi Saloon*, he gives us a hero worth admiring: the passive, overweight, depressed and sex-obsessed Harry Hudson, who in the face of almost overwhelming despair still manages to lead a valorous life of deep faith. In this powerful and compelling first novel, Harris makes roses bloom in the gray underworld of porno shops, bars and brothels by compassionately revealing the yearning loneliness beneath the grime—our universal human loneliness that seeks transcendence through love." — Paula Huston, author of *Daughters of Song* and *The Holy Way*

"*The Chieu Hoi Saloon* concerns one Harry Hudson, the literary bastard son of David Goodis and Dorothy Hughes. Hardcore and unsparing, the story takes you on a ride with Harry in his bucket of a car and pulls you into his subterranean existence in bright daylight and gloomy shadow. One sweet read." — Gary Phillips, author of *The Jook*

Pike
Benjamin Whitmer
ISBN: 978-1-60486-089-4
224 pages $15.95

Douglas Pike is no longer the murderous hustler he was
in his youth, but reforming hasn't made him much kinder.
He's just living out his life in his Appalachian hometown,
working odd jobs with his partner, Rory, hemming in his
demons the best he can. And his best seems just good
enough until his estranged daughter overdoses and he takes
in his twelve-year-old granddaughter, Wendy.

Just as the two are beginning to forge a relationship, Derrick Kreiger, a dirty Cincinnati
cop, starts to take an unhealthy interest in the girl. Pike and Rory head to Cincinnati to
learn what they can about Derrick and the death of Pike's daughter, and the three men
circle, evenly matched predators in a human wilderness of junkie squats, roadhouse
bars and homeless Vietnam vet encampments.

"Without so much as a sideways glance towards gentility, *Pike* is one righteous
mutherfucker of a read. I move that we put Whitmer's balls in a vise and keep slowly
notching up the torque until he's willing to divulge the secret of how he managed to
hit such a perfect stride his first time out of the blocks." — Ward Churchill

"Benjamin Whitmer's *Pike* captures the grime and the rage of my not-so-fair city
with disturbing precision. The words don't just tell a story here, they scream, bleed,
and burst into flames. *Pike*, like its eponymous main character, is a vicious punisher
that doesn't mince words or take prisoners, and no one walks away unscathed. This
one's going to haunt me for quite some time." — Nathan Singer

"This is what noir is, what it can be when it stops playing nice — blunt force drama
stripped down to the bone, then made to dance across the page." — Stephen Graham
Jones

I-5
Summer Brenner
ISBN: 978-1-60486-019-1
256 pages $15.95

A novel of crime, transport, and sex, *I-5* tells the bleak and brutal story of Anya and her journey north from Los Angeles to Oakland on the interstate that bisects the Central Valley of California.

Anya is the victim of a deep deception. Someone has lied to her; and because of this lie, she is kept under lock and key, used by her employer to service men, and indebted for the privilege. In exchange, she lives in the United States and fantasizes on a future American freedom. Or as she remarks to a friend, "Would she rather be fucking a dog... or living like a dog?" In Anya's world, it's a reasonable question.

Much of *I-5* transpires on the eponymous interstate. Anya travels with her "manager" and driver from Los Angeles to Oakland. It's a macabre journey: a drop at Denny's, a bad patch of fog, a visit to a "correctional facility," a rendezvous with an organ grinder, and a dramatic entry across Oakland's city limits.

"Insightful, innovative and riveting. After its lyrical beginning inside Anya's head, *I-5* shifts momentum into a rollicking gangsters-on-the-lam tale that is in turns blackly humorous, suspenseful, heartbreaking and always populated by intriguing characters. Anya is a wonderful, believable heroine, her tragic tale told from the inside out, without a shred of sentimental pity, which makes it all the stronger. A twisty, fast-paced ride you won't soon forget." — Denise Hamilton, author of the *L.A. Times* bestseller *The Last Embrace*.

"I'm in awe. *I-5* moves so fast you can barely catch your breath. It's as tough as tires, as real and nasty as road rage, and best of all, it careens at breakneck speed over as many twists and turns as you'll find on The Grapevine. What a ride! *I-5*'s a hard-boiled standout." — Julie Smith, editor of *New Orleans Noir* and author of the Skip Langdon and Talba Wallis crime novel series

"In *I-5*, Summer Brenner deals with the onerous and gruesome subject of sex trafficking calmly and forcefully, making the reader feel the pain of its victims. The trick to forging a successful narrative is always in the details, and *I-5* provides them in abundance. This book bleeds truth — after you finish it, the blood will be on your hands." — Barry Gifford, author, poet and screenwriter